ACT OF GOD

ACT OF GOD

Jill Ciment

Pantheon · New York

Copyright © 2015 by Jill Ciment

All rights reserved. Published in the United States by
Pantheon Books, a division of Random House LLC, New York,
and in Canada by Random House of Canada Limited, Toronto,
Penguin Random House companies.

Pantheon Books and colophon are registered trademarks of
Random House LLC.

Library of Congress Cataloging-in-Publication Data
Ciment, Jill, [date]
Act of god / Jill Ciment.
pages   cm
ISBN 978-0-307-91170-4 (hardback)
ISBN 978-0-307-91171-1 (eBook)
1. Mold (Fungi)—Fiction.   2. New York (N.Y.)—Fiction.
I. Title.
PR9199.3.C499A28   2015   813'.54—dc23   2014012087

www.pantheonbooks.com

Jacket images: (details) CSA Images / Getty Images;
(top right) © csaimages.com
Jacket design by Janet Hansen

Printed in the United States of America
First Edition

1   3   5   7   9   8   6   4   2

For Arnold

In memory of my mother, Gloria Ciment

PART ONE

TILL HELL FREEZES OVER

The twins suspected it was alive, but they weren't exactly sure if it was plant or animal.

Edith, white-haired and older by seventeen minutes, went to find a flashlight while Kat, blond with white roots, knelt to take a closer look. A small phosphorescent organism, about as bright and arresting as a firefly's glow, bloomed in the seam of the hall closet. It almost looked as if someone had chewed a piece of iridescence and stuck it, like gum, on the wall. But it wasn't inanimate like gum; its surface was roiling as if something beneath were struggling to be born. Kat tried to call Edith back to be assured that she wasn't imagining things, but Kat was struck dumb. A swell rose out of the glow until the head of whatever was fighting to get born pushed through, a fleshy bud, about the size of a newborn's thumb. Kat gasped. Her breath must have disturbed the new life, or awakened it, because a puff of spores sprayed out, luminous and ephemeral as glitter. The closet housed their mother's archives, the original letters from her advice column, the earliest dating back to the nineteen fifties, when Consultations with Dr. Mimi was first syndicated. All they needed was for spores to land on one of the file boxes and start feasting on the invaluable old papers inside.

Edith shined the flashlight over Kat's shoulder. They could now see clearly that it wasn't a plant or an animal. It was some kind of mushroom, a fleshy speckled stalk capped by a deeply oxygenated pink head. Edith gasped. They sounded identical.

"Where did it come from?" Edith's voice quavered between stubborn disbelief and reverent horror. "How does a mushroom just start growing out of a wall, or is it growing *through* the wall? Oh my god, what's behind it? You shouldn't be so close, Kat. It may be poisonous." She kept the light trained on it, as if the mushroom were under interrogation.

They decided not to touch anything until they spoke to someone with expertise in these matters. But who would that be? Who do you call? The Health Department, Pest Control, the EPA, the CDC, the Fire Department? Should they call the super?

But they both knew what Frank would do—nothing. He'd gawk at the mushroom, sympathize, light a cigarette, even though Edith asked him not to smoke around the archive, and then call their landlady, Vida Cebu. Vida was an actress who had bought the building last year, a narrow, three-story, neoclassic row house on Berry Street in Brooklyn. She had restored the warren of dwellings above Edith's apartment into a private house again, but she could do nothing about the parlor floor. Edith had inherited their mother's rent-controlled lease—a tenant till death. And now Kat had moved in. Edith paid two hundred dollars and twelve cents a month.

While Kat peeked over Edith's shoulder, Edith typed *mushrooms, brooklyn* into her computer's search engine, but the only listings were gourmet stores selling truffles and porcinis.

"Isn't a mushroom a type of mold?" Kat asked.

Big Apple Mold, Terminix, Mold Be Gone, Ecology Exter-

minating Service, Basement RX, Empire Disaster Restoration.
Who would have guessed there were so many mold special-
ists in their zip code? After the tenth answering machine, the
twins realized that everybody was closed for the weekend. It
was two o'clock, Sunday afternoon. Edith dialed the only
one with an after-hours number.

"Mold Be Gone," a woman answered.

"Thank god someone's there. We found a mushroom
growing in our closet. What should we do?"

"I only work for the answering service, but I'd pour
bleach on it and keep your air conditioner on high. Someone will call you Monday."

The window units were already running at full tilt, and
had been since the heat wave began twenty-six days ago. The
temperature had broken last year's record by two degrees.
People were fainting in the streets.

The first thing the twins did was rescue their mother's
archives. Sixteen heavy boxes weren't easy to move.

"It's grown, hasn't it?" Edith said breathlessly, staring
back into the empty closet.

The mushroom now stood upright and had tripled in
size.

Bleach might not kill it, but surely it would stunt its
growth. Edith found a Clorox bottle under the kitchen
sink, Kat rubber gloves in the bathroom. Before uncapping
the bleach, they tied handkerchiefs around their noses and
mouths. The fumes immediately saturated the tight space.
Eyes smarting, Edith tipped the bottle's spout directly over
the mushroom while Kat held a large tin foil roasting pan
underneath to catch the runoff. When the first drops hit,
the mushroom must have sensed its fate. Its gills shrank
closed. Edith kept pouring. The thick stalk started going
flaccid. The pink head lost its blush. She finished the bottle.

The roasting pan was now a tub of bleach. Kat set it on the floor, under the obviously dying mushroom.

They watched its demise with profound relief. The more it withered and shriveled, the calmer they became. It shrank even faster than it had grown. Finally, it just hung by a tendril.

"I'm going to pull it off," Kat said.

"Don't touch it. I'll get a knife," Edith said.

The blade barely scratched the skin before the mushroom fell into the roasting pan.

They inspected the corner. The wall looked surprisingly clean, except for a pale spore print in the seam, but even that seemed superficial. They scraped it away with the point of the knife. The mushroom had only been stuck, not rooted, to the wall.

They scrubbed the area three separate times, with bleach, with rubbing alcohol, with antibacterial dish soap, and finally, Edith sprayed Raid on it. Before cleaning up, Edith turned off the lights in the hall closet and shut herself inside to hunt for any luminous pinpricks of overlooked spores. Satisfied they'd eradicated all they could find, she and Kat carried out the roasting pan and dumped its contents in the gutter, including the now shriveled twist of fungus.

They returned to the apartment. The closet had never looked so clean. It almost seemed as if they'd imagined the mushroom.

"That was disturbing," Edith said. "My god, it grew freakishly fast. The head was so pink and bulbous. It almost looked like a giant's thumb had poked through the wall."

Kat waited to see if Edith would draw the obvious analogy, but she wasn't sure if her white-haired, sixty-four-year-old sister had ever seen an erect penis. She suspected Edith was a virgin. The not knowing was an inscrutable power

Edith held over her. All their lives, Kat had told Edith the most intimate details about her lovers and escapades, whereas Edith confided nothing to her. All Kat knew was that Edith, before retiring, had worked in one of those anthill corporate law firms as the head librarian and lived with their mother until she died. Had Edith had a secret lover, perhaps one of the married partners? Surely Edith had been in love once or twice? Had she ever been caressed? Kissed? When they were children, Edith and Kat looked identical. But by their early twenties, you could barely tell they were twins. Edith was stout, Kat voluptuous. Edith kept her original brown hair color; Kat changed hers as often as she fell in love. It wasn't just the physical differences. Their identical countenances expressed two very different souls. Edith wore their features sensibly and wisely; Kat gave them sparkle and animation. But these days, sharing the same clothes, the same meals, they again looked identical. Or did they? Kat had only seen her sister naked once since she'd moved in two months ago, when she had to help Edith bathe after a bad bout of flu. Edith's skin looked almost translucent compared to her own freckled, sun-damaged hide, but otherwise they'd aged with remarkable similarity. Sponging her likeness, all Kat could think was that this was what she would have looked like had she never allowed herself to live and be loved.

Edith phoned Vida to report the infestation, while Kat returned to what she'd been doing before she had seen the disturbing bloom in the closet. She'd been going through their mother's archives, assembling *The Best of Consultations with Dr. Mimi* before Edith shipped the original letters to their permanent home at the Smithsonian next month. The archivist there was a friend of Edith's, and they'd planned a small exhibition in one of the libraries to mark the event. The book had been Kat's idea, to give the enterprise a little pizzazz. If only Edith would put aside her doubts. Sutton House Publishers had already expressed interest. Their mother's advice column had been wildly popular in the nineteen sixties, an epistolary history of the burgeoning sexual revolution, running daily in over a hundred newspapers. Their mother was the first to call body parts and functions by their real names and answer sexual questions with nonjudgmental, instructional advice. Each letter began with "Dear Dr. Mimi" and ended with a surprisingly frank emotion and a place to call home: "Ashamed in Nebraska," "Wicked in the Bronx." In between the salutations and the sign-offs, raw, guileless, enraged, mortified, slighted, embittered, sly, self-delusional, self-pitying, blunt, kind, dejected, heartbroken, and heartrending voices asked questions about the inexplicable behavior of lovers, boyfriends, crushes, flirts, husbands, other men's wives, other wives' husbands, all their fellow creatures. It hardly mattered whether the question had been composed with a blunt pencil on a greasy brown bag or with a fountain pen on Plaza stationery, the letters basically asked the same thing—*Am I lovable?*

Kat knew that Edith dismissed her book project as just another excuse not to look for a job. The last few years had been lean and scary. Kat's soap-making business had dissolved; then she'd lost her booth at the Eugene farmer's market, and spent the fall living in a campground trailer amid the California redwoods. She'd met a fascinating crew—mystics and migrants who picked the marijuana crop—and it had been glorious living in a prehistoric forest until winter came. Even then, when the ocean fog clapped against the frigid air and shrouded the mile-high treetops, the behemoth trunks looked as if they were holding up heaven.

Kat regretted nothing about her life—not the many lovers, both gracious and brutish, not the failed sturgeon farm in New Mexico or the soap fiasco in Oregon, not the years as a Deadhead, not the singing lessons or the political street theater, not the exalted clarity of acid or the cheery bliss of alcohol. Only this: when they were girls, Edith had worshipped her, and now she pitied her.

Edith left an urgent message on Vida's voicemail knowing beforehand that Vida wouldn't answer. She never did when she saw Edith's number flashing on her phone. Last week, Edith had left four messages about the fetid odor in the laundry room and another when the foul smell permeated the rear garden. Vida had been home the whole time. Edith had heard her sharp footsteps clatter across the ceiling.

Edith left Kat making a mess of the orderly archives and went downstairs to check for water leaks. The bulk of the letters were stored in the basement, hermetically sealed in double-strength plastic boxes.

The cellar was always jungle hot in August, but that Sunday, after three and a half weeks of hundred-plus temperatures, Edith felt as if she were descending into a live volcano. The ceiling was veined with old pipes, but none appeared to be leaking. She checked the archive boxes for any signs of mold, but the plastic appeared clean, the seals unbroken. Then she shut off the lights and stood in the hellish heat, looking heavenward. A small eternity passed before her vision adapted, but gradually dozens and dozens of luminous pinpricks perforated the darkness overhead. She couldn't tell if the stars were growing bigger and brighter or if her pupils had finally adjusted. Whatever was blooming on the ceiling didn't need a leak for sustenance.

Back upstairs, she left another message on Vida's voicemail. "It's me again, pick up, I know you're there. We have a mold infestation in the basement. Kat and I found a mushroom growing in our hall closet this morning. I don't have to tell you how disturbing all this is. Phone me."

After she hung up, she stayed in her bedroom, alone, the door shut, her only sanctuary from Kat. Three months ago, she'd retired after thirty years as head librarian at Price, Bloodworth, Flom, Mead & Van Doren. She'd taken immense satisfaction in her work over the years, attaining a near-omniscient knowledge of New York tort law, but the recent digitalization of her beloved legal tomes and the increasing stress on billable hours had decided her. She had just begun to enjoy the quietude and attend to a few personal projects, such as the Smithsonian exhibition of her mother's archive, when Kat called late one night from the Port Authority bus terminal, asking to spend the night. Two months later, Kat still occupied the guest room with no prospects of affording her own place, unless *Dr. Mimi's Greatest Hits* or whatever she called her book became a best seller. Edith had Googled Sutton House. They published novelty books. Her poor delusional sister had always mistaken irresponsibility for daring, eccentricity for originality, obsession for intimacy. That first night, when Edith opened the door for her bedraggled sister, Kat looked blurrier, as if she had become a poor, faded copy of her former self. Edith hadn't seen her in nearly a year. She was dressed in her usual bangles and bright scarves, but everything about her looked smudged, except her blinding new smile. She'd had her front incisors capped in brilliant porcelain. Two big white tombstones in a graveyard of antique canines and molars. The dentist must have suggested a tamer white, something more muted that might have better blended in, but her crazy sister must have insisted, *I want the biggest brightest teeth you have.*

Edith's skin felt hot and clammy from the basement. Her air conditioner rattled in the window, but its cold breath brought little relief, a flower vase of water thrown on a grease fire. There were twelve thousand BTUs of cold air blowing through the apartment, but Vida had registered the building as a historic site and all street-facing units had had to be removed. The front half of the apartment, including the infested hall closet, was stifling.

Sitting at her desk, Edith woke her computer. She wanted to identify the mushroom so that she could describe it accurately to the exterminators tomorrow. She typed—*mold, fungi, bioluminous, rapid propagation, lack of water source*—into the search engine, then clicked on images. Her screen filled with countless pictures of glowing mushrooms sprouting from walls, baseboards, acoustic ceilings, toilets, shower tiles, bathtub grout, drains, light fixtures, and a piano.

She didn't usually read blogs or enter chat rooms, but that Sunday she found herself visiting websites devoted to every fear man experienced when the kingdom of fungi bloomed in his castle. She watched a YouTube video of a luminescent mushroom growing out of an electric socket while a baritone male voice with a Brooklyn accent kept incanting, "Holy shit, mother of god, holy shit . . ."

His mushroom looked just like theirs. Or did it?

She read the comments below the video, though she knew what kind of hysterics and bullies posted opinions online.

bobandbarb: don't call the New York City Health department, whatever you do, we made that mistake when we found the first glowing mushroom under our bed, and now we're living in our truck.

Flatstomach886: ewwwwwwwwwww. boo hoo!

grandmafairy: Don't wait for the mushrooms to appear. Look for signs of memory loss and pulmonary hemorrhage. If you have symptoms for which the doctors cannot find a cause, I advise you to get out now.

prozacbaby: Just yesterday I tried to lie down for a nap and suddenly this overwhelming smell filled the room, it wasn't making me gag but it made me get really scared. It smelled the way my grandfather smelled at the funeral home. Will I die soon? We've got mushrooms.

rollitup: does it smell like a faggot's fart? faggot farts glow.

blazingwaffles: They burned down my rowhouse! Do you know who burned it down? The Brooklyn Fire department. Do you think your insurance will pay? Think again. Mushrooms are an act of God according to AllState.

Edith left another urgent voicemail, all the while listening, with mounting fury, to Vida's footsteps overhead.

Vida suspected that Frank, her super, had been sneaking into her apartment and snooping through her things while she was on location. Nothing was ever missing, nothing she could be certain about. Her jewelry was always accounted for. Her spare cash lay untouched in her underwear drawer. Yet something felt amiss. The cash might not have been touched, but her panties were definitely fingered. Someone had neatly folded them, and it wasn't her. Or was it? Had she folded them? She'd never folded panties in her life. Her entire apartment seemed too clean, as if in her absence, all evidence of life, including her own, had been swept up or scrubbed away. The banister was dustless, the tub spotless, the sheets changed. Had she changed them before she left? No, someone had been in here and had cleaned up after himself with a little too much rigor.

Vida suspected Frank not only because he wielded the building's master key. Frank also gave her the *grin*, a licentious spellbound leer, as if he were privy to her erotic aches. He wasn't the only man who looked at her that way, but he was the only one with keys to her apartment. Ever since she'd made the Ziberax commercial, old men had treated her with courtly craving, and young men with blatant want.

In the commercial, she played a fortyish businesswoman who appeared to have everything—a lovely rambling beach house, her own fashion line, a sexy gray-templed husband who adored her. But the brittleness with which she responded to his playful kisses betrayed her unhappiness. Until her doctor prescribed Ziberax, her sex was as cold and lifeless as plastic.

To introduce the first female sexual enhancement pill, a pink oval tablet, to its target audience—college-educated women between forty and sixty whose husbands or boyfriends already took erectile dysfunction pills—the admen had wanted an especially sexy actress on the kind side of middle age, more striking than pretty, an earned beauty. During the audition, the director had asked Vida to imagine her first satisfying orgasm in years; she's now in her lover's arms, and her expression should exude not just sexual bliss—although that too—but also reawakened intimacy. To achieve a look of fulfillment so cellular that it melded her soul with another's, Vida relaxed the muscles of her face until her expression became as still, and deep, and mysterious as well water.

She'd fire Frank today, but she had no proof. He'd been the apartment building's super for over thirty years before she came along and restored it to a single house again, except for the rent-controlled parlor floor. She phoned the police to see what they'd advise. After she enumerated her suspicions about Frank, the desk officer asked her what was missing.

"Nothing's missing," she said. "But my panties have been folded."

"You think your super's folding your underwear?"

"Yes, and I want to know what can be done about it."

"Without more evidence, all you can do is request a squad car drive-by once a night to make sure no one's breaking in."

"He's the super. He has the key."

Her agent and lawyer and oldest friend in New York, Virginia, a harried single mother of a clingy toddler, suggested a security firm she used to spy on her son's nanny, Peace of Mind Technologies. "They set up hidden cameras throughout the apartment and I caught the little Russian sociopath on video giving Zacky an Ambien!"

The young man from the security firm recommended a dozen nannycams with silent-alarm motion detectors that would automatically alert the police if an intruder was present. "Do you have children?"

"Why?"

"The nannycams are usually concealed in toys, but we also have a pencil sharpener, an alarm clock, and a smoke detector model."

After the tech left the next day, and Vida was alone with the pencil sharpener, the alarm clock, and the smoke detector, she wondered who was watching her. Her plan was to leave early the next morning, but not so early that Frank didn't see her go. He was perpetually sweeping someone's sidewalk. He lived on the block, though she couldn't say exactly where. He seemed to have keys to all the buildings. The neighbors called him the "mayor of Berry Street," though he looked more like an ex-prizefighter than a politician. He once told Vida that in his sixty-four years, he'd been to Manhattan less than a dozen times.

"Where you off to now? Hollywood calling?" Frank shouted from across the street, broom in hand. He gave her the *grin.*

"I'll be back on Thursday. Keep an eye on things," she said, wheeling a small suitcase behind her. It wasn't just a prop; she'd packed a few things in case Frank didn't take the bait right away and she had to spend the night at a hotel.

"Is it a comedy?"

"It's a police thriller, Frank."

About an hour later, killing time in a nearby coffee shop, she got the call. "Peace of Mind Technologies," said a prerecorded voice, "the police are on their way."

Two squad cars, red lights awhirl, were double-parked in front of her row house. The refurbished Victorian front door had been crowbarred open, its original oval glass shattered. Her tenant Edith and her twin sister Kat leaned out the front window, talking to Frank. If Frank was downstairs, who was upstairs? "What happened?" she asked.

"A burglary was in progress so the police had to smash down your front door," said Frank.

"Did you get my messages? We have a mold infestation," said Edith.

Vida stepped over the glass shards. A policewoman stood sentry just inside the foyer. "The landlady's here," she said into her walkie-talkie.

Vida mounted the steep staircase. Her apartment door hung wide open. She heard voices coming from inside, a deep, officious male and a brazen, Slavic-accented female. Even with the policewoman beside her, Vida paused before going in. The policeman, who didn't look a day over twenty, stood in her living room arguing with a small, very pretty young woman about his age. Her shoulder-length black hair was wet from the shower and tied in a ponytail. She sported a Ziberax promotional T-shirt that Vida had thought she'd thrown away, a pair of Vida's lace panties, and handcuffs.

"Do you know her?" asked the policewoman.

"Who is she?"

"She says she lives here."

"I've never seen her before in my life."

"We found her hiding in the closet." The policewoman pointed toward the guest room, a storage room, really. Vida couldn't remember the last time she'd been in there. "She says she's been living here a week."

"That's impossible," Vida said.

"You didn't notice anything? We found her bedding."

"Oh my god, this is so creepy. She's been here a week! Get her out, now," Vida said.

"We need to collect the bedding as evidence."

"Be my guest," Vida said, as the policewoman disappeared into the guest room.

"Please I keep my things?" the pretty prisoner asked the boy officer. Vida could now distinguish the accent, throaty Russian. The girl had changed her strategy: instead of arguing, she now flirted with her guard.

"We'll bag them for you, miss, and you can collect them when you're released."

"You're going to release her? What if she comes back?"

"I steal nothing," the pretty prisoner told the boy officer. "She left downstairs door open."

The policewoman called to Vida from the guest room. "There's a lot of stuff in the closet. I don't know whose is whose."

Vida dreaded going in there. She didn't want to know what, exactly, the officer had meant by *bedding*. It was a storage closet filled with clothes she never wore. She was hardly about to start wearing them now.

"Take everything," Vida called back.

"Red suitcase is mine," the pretty prisoner whispered under her breath, forcing the boy officer to lean close, close enough to smell her skin.

Vida hesitantly entered the guest room. It had never looked cleaner. The closet light was on. Vida's wardrobe had been parted, like theater curtains, swept to either end of the hanger rod, revealing a camp of sorts. The bedding, which she'd dreaded seeing, was a clean white comforter and fairly new rose-patterned sheets. Vida only bought solid colors. Near the pillow, suited in a matching floral pillowcase, stood the guest room's gooseneck lamp. Arranged around the lamp's base, as if on a vanity table, lay a brush, a tube of lipstick, an emery board, and a paperback, *The New Earth: Awakening Your Life's Purpose.*

When Vida, speechless, failed to instruct the policewoman as to what belonged to whom, the prisoner took charge. "Linens are mine, but not pillow. Lamp not mine, but book and brush is. Also, I have shoes."

Wearing latex gloves, the policewoman bagged the linens, sundries, and a pair of high heels.

"Don't forget suitcase," the prisoner reminded the boy officer. Bound in handcuffs, she used her lovely chin to point even deeper into the closet, under Vida's swept-aside hems. The policeboy had to crawl on hands and knees. "Marie," he called to his partner, "take a look at this."

Ordering the prisoner not to move, the policewoman joined him in the closet.

Alone with the prisoner, Vida suddenly found her voice. "How long were you planning on staying? You thought I wouldn't notice a stranger living in my house? What did you use for a bathroom when I was home? I don't want to know." Vida looked back at the closet. The naked pillow and the gooseneck lamp had been set aside for her—as if she'd want them now. She'd call Goodwill tomorrow and have them take everything away. Then she'd call one of those special crime scene cleaning services.

"Ma'am, have you seen this before?" asked the policewoman, signaling her over.

Reluctantly, Vida stuck her head in the closet. She noticed the pale, otherworldly glow only after the boy officer pointed it out. It appeared to be emanating from a bulge in the wall. The policewoman shined her flashlight on it. "Oh my god, is that a mushroom?" Vida reeled around and shouted at the prisoner, "What have you been doing in there?!"

"It already there when I move in."

No one had to tell the twins that this wasn't an ordinary break-in. In addition to the police cars, a fire truck now blocked the street, HAZMAT lettered across its bright red side. Still in her bathrobe, eating a corn muffin with her coffee, Kat watched from the parlor's bay window, while Edith, showered and dressed, sat at her desk phoning an exterminator.

"What's a biohazard response team doing at a burglary?" Kat wondered out loud.

Edith walked over to see for herself. "Maybe it has to do with the mold infestation," she said, opening the window. She called to the firemen, "Are we safe? Should we leave?"

"Stay where you are for the moment," said the chief. He wore yellow-slicker coveralls, rubber gloves, and disposable booties, but unlike his crew of six, he didn't have on his respirator. It dangled from a strap around his neck.

Frank and a small flock of curious neighbors stood cordoned off behind a squad car, its front doors open like wings.

"Who called the HAZMAT team?" Edith shouted to him.

"Not me. I've never seen a truck like that in my life."

"Maybe the burglar had bird flu?" suggested Gladys, the neighbor who lived next door with her seventeen cats.

"The lady cop told me the burglar was sleeping in Vida's

guest room without Vida even knowing," Frank told the twins.

"For how long?" called Kat.

"Long enough."

Someone knocked at the door.

"Ladies, we're going to need you to vacate," said the policewoman, now wearing what looked like a house painter's mask. "Toxic mold has been found in your landlady's closet. At the very least, the building will need to be fumigated. Make sure you take all your important papers."

"We have thousands of important papers, we have a historical archive in here," said Edith.

"Just take what you need for now."

Edith hurried to her desk to collect her BlackBerry and purse. She packed an overnight bag with a change of clothes, sundries, and a copy of her insurance policy. Then she reached under the bed to retrieve the shoe box where she kept their mother's original rent-controlled lease. Even before she raised the lid, she saw a faint greenish luminosity emanating from underneath. A mushroom was feeding on the ancient document. With a tremor of fear so elemental that it shivered all the way back to childhood, she lifted the bed skirt and peeked underneath. The rug was stained with iridescent drips, as if phosphorescence had leaked from the mattress. She looked up. Another mushroom sprouted from the bed frame.

Meanwhile, Kat sat immobilized in the second bedroom, Edith's former office, on her unmade bed. The three-ring binder, thick with her mother's most promising letters, was the first and only possession she had definitively set aside to save. The rest of her belongings—T-shirts, a washed-out batik sari, stretched-out underwear, yoga pants, sandals, and a Goodwill winter coat—seemed almost foolish to save, except for her beloved scarves, each bought in a different city. Should she pack the pantsuit that Edith gave her to wear for job interviews? Would remembering to pack the suit finally convince Edith that she was serious about job hunting as soon as the book was finished?

What else should she take?

Edith appeared in the doorway. "You're not dressed yet? You're not packed? They're telling us we've got to get out of here, *now*!"

"Let me get this straight, *she* breaks into my house and *I* have to get out?" asked Vida, incredulous.

"Everyone has to leave. Your downstairs tenants have already been evacuated," explained the policewoman, her voice commanding despite the mask covering her mouth and nose.

"Why not I get mask?" demanded the pretty prisoner, wildly indignant, as only those speaking with Russian cadences can sound. Still in handcuffs, she sat perched on the sofa's arm, bare legs crossed, while the boy officer stood behind her at military at-ease.

Vida couldn't help but admire the girl's moxie. Then she remembered the bedding in the closet, and a shiver of revulsion jolted her, as if the white comforter and the clean sheets had been a rat's nest. "When can I return?" she asked the masked officer. "Tonight? Tomorrow? How many nights are we talking about?"

"Just pack what you'll need for now," said the policewoman.

Vida already had the packed overnight bag for her ruse to catch Frank. She had made a reservation at the Lohito Grand, a thirty-story aquamarine whale breaching the

Lower East Side tenements. She went upstairs to her office, directly above the guest room, retrieved her laptop, and then stopped by her bedroom to collect the emergency cash she kept in her underwear drawer. Only when she saw the neatly folded panties did it occur to her: *she* had worn them all. Why couldn't she have just stolen the cash and the jewelry and then run away, like a normal thief?

Vida glanced back at the guest room on her way out. The pretty prisoner now stood over the boy officer. Fumbling through her open red suitcase, he was trying to find her something to wear over Vida's lace panties. On the street, Vida followed the policewoman over to the squad car. Frank and the nosy neighbors crowded around the twins. Normally, whenever Frank saw Vida, he gave her the *grin*. Not today. He looked right past her. The pretty prisoner was making her slow descent down the stoop steps, escorted by the policeboy as if she were being debuted at a cotillion wearing a white gown rather than being arrested in skintight pink Capris. Her shoulder-length black hair was loose and wild. She was still in handcuffs. Who let the ponytail down? Vida recognized the girl's gait, an amateur's stage walk, every brazen sway designed to hide fright. Vida had used that exact same gait for her first audition, Tess, the rebellious daughter, in the off-Broadway production of *Six Degrees of Separation*. In those days, Vida still went by her given name, Debbi. Her parents, a Filipina dental hygienist and an Irish locksmith, had thought it was the American spelling.

"You'll need to come to the station if you want to press charges," said the policewoman.

"How long will that take? Please, can't you just drive her to another neighborhood so that she doesn't come back?"

"You can get a restraining order to keep her a thousand feet from your house, but you'll still need to come in."

"What's she charged with?"

"Criminal trespass."

"That's all? She'll be out tomorrow."

"We can charge her with first-degree burglary if you think she's stolen anything."

The only items that Vida could prove had been taken were the Ziberax T-shirt and the lace panties. Vida preferred not to have to testify in court, *I'm the Ziberax lady and that's my T-shirt and those are my panties.* "Let her go," Vida said.

"Are you sure?"

Vida made one last assessment of the prisoner, who was standing defiantly under the fierce sun as if under a hot spotlight; the girl was well aware that she held the rapt attention of her audience. A professional at reading and conveying expressions, Vida also noted that the girl's rebellious insouciance was one exhalation short of panic.

"Let her go, but warn her that if I see her again, anywhere near here, I'm pressing charges." Despite the nonstop chatter coming from the squad car radio, when the policewoman removed the handcuffs and told her she was free, Vida heard the prisoner's response.

"Where are sheets and pillowcase?"

Wheeling her suitcase behind her, Vida approached the fire chief. "What happens next?" she asked as calmly as she could manage.

"The city temporarily condemns your building."

"And?"

"And you fumigate."

"Who do I contact?"

"I'd phone my insurance company and find out what your mold coverage is. If you're covered, your agent will suggest a fumigator." His expression remained officious, but Vida noticed the spark of recognition in his eyes. His face suddenly changed from stoic commander to charmed admirer as he struggled to hold back the *grin*.

"Who else should I be calling?" she asked.

"I'd call my lawyer," he said, unable to contain the *grin* any longer.

Before she could reach for her cell phone, Edith strode toward her. When Vida first bought the building, she had tried to buy out all the tenants, made them generous offers, more than the realtor had recommended. Only Edith had said no and never made a counter offer. Maybe she could buy her out now?

"I left five urgent messages and you never called me back. I warned you last week that a foul odor was coming from the laundry room," Edith began, barely able to control her rage. "Now we have a catastrophe on our hands. I found a mushroom growing under my bed. All the furniture will need to be thrown out and burned. And what about my mother's archive? Can you promise me that the fungicide won't destroy the letters? When can we expect to go home?"

"I wish I knew. No one's telling me anything either," Vida said.

Edith didn't believe her. In her summer dress and sandals, Vida must have charmed an answer or two out of the fire chief. He practically had to wrestle his eyes off her before returning to duty. "What are we supposed to do in the meantime? Where are we supposed to live?"

"I don't know what to say. I'm out on the street myself."

A sedan navigated around the emergency vehicles and pulled up to the curb. Wheeling her suitcase behind her, Vida got in. When did she have time to call a car service? Edith wondered. She watched Vida settle in the rear seat, subsiding into the cool interior. Before the tinted window rose, Edith called, "I expect to hear from you this afternoon, or you'll hear from my lawyer."

She looked around for Kat, but Kat wasn't where she was

supposed to be, guarding their luggage and purses as Edith had asked. Kat was waving good-bye to the newly released prisoner.

"You know her?"

"Ashley? I thought she was Vida's maid. We met in the garden. She said hello and introduced herself. What kind of a burglar introduces herself?"

Gripping the hot iron banister, Edith eased herself down on Gladys's stoop, which was thick with cat hair. The noon sun smoldered directly overhead. The air felt unusually still, as if the morning had run out of breath. Her anger rapidly evaporated into despair. She remembered what she'd forgotten to pack in her haste—her heart medication. And she hadn't washed her hands since she'd touched the infested shoe box.

Kat joined her on the steps. The humidity had varnished Kat's permanent suntan resin yellow. Her blond wisps lay sweat-plastered to her scalp, dead cornstalks rain-beaten on the ground. She hadn't had time to put on her makeup, and her eyes looked naked and vulnerable.

"Where are we supposed to go?" Edith said out loud to herself.

Kat gently guided Edith's chin until they faced each other. Looking directly into Kat's eyes was both greatly comforting and oddly disquieting to Edith. They were born with matching pale blue irises down to the coronas of forest green around the pupils, but over time, Kat's dark nimbuses had widened, leaving an impression that her stare vectored just beyond this world. She smiled reassuringly at Edith with her zealous teeth.

"Edie, we're going to be fine. We'll treat ourselves to a nice hotel," she said, as if their eviction was cause for celebration and she was picking up the tab.

The policewoman came over and took off her painter's mask. Edith was surprised to see that a policewoman wore lipstick. "Do you ladies have someone to call? Anyplace to stay tonight?"

Edith could have phoned one of her old friends from work, but Maggie had just moved in with her daughter and Janice lived in a small one-bedroom. Janice might have been able to squeeze in one, but two?

"Any family?" asked the policewoman.

Neither twin had married or had children.

"No," Edith said.

"Do you need public assistance? Would you like to speak to a caseworker from the Department of Aging?"

"The Department of *Aging*? We'll get a hotel, thank you very much," said Kat.

Edith couldn't conceal her exasperation. Kat was more indignant about being labeled "aging" than she was about their being temporarily homeless.

Kat knew that Edith thought she was in denial about growing old, but the blond hair and the suntan weren't feeble attempts to mask the truth; they were medals. Had she let herself age like Edith, without a struggle, her body wouldn't reflect her being. She would no more be herself with white hair than if she sported a barrister's wig. Her carriage and stride were still nimble and lithe. She had never stopped believing that she was on the brink of hurling herself into something significant.

Edith found them a room at the Metropolitan, a two-star neighborhood hotel with a twelve-lane view of the Brooklyn-Queens Expressway. The room was barely large enough to hold two single beds, a suitcase rack, and a coffeemaker. Kat showered first, then sprawled naked on her sheets, her shampooed hair damp and turbaned in a towel. From her pillow facing the curtained window, the expressway appeared to converge at her bare feet.

Pallid and blotchy, Edith sat on the opposite bed, still wearing her sweaty, sticky street clothes. Strands of white hair clung to her gleaming brow as if chalked on. The low late-afternoon sun sliced through the curtains and blanched her to the bones, turned her dress to ectoplasm and her hair to transient smoke, leaving only the essence of her bearing, an austere armature.

Kat was terribly worried about Edith. The blotches meant that Edith's blood pressure had spiked again.

"She should have called by now," Edith said.

"Who?"

"Vida. I'm going over there to see if Frank knows anything and then stop by the pharmacy. I left my heart medicine on the nightstand."

"Edie, you're going to give yourself a stroke. Take a shower, cool off, and lie down. I'll go."

Their block, normally a human anthill on a summer evening, was eerily deserted. The steam-bath heat was keeping everyone indoors. The only reminder that Kat saw of today's four-alarm response was a cat's cradle of yellow police tape tying off their stoop and a Health Department vacate order stapled to the doorjamb at eye level.

Frank emerged from Gladys's basement hauling out two overstuffed transparent recycling bags, cat food tins rattling within like maracas. At sixty-four, he still had the jacked arms of a pugilist. Kat was both relieved and comforted to see him attending to everyday chores. They'd known each other for more than forty years. Before Frank was a super, he'd been a welterweight boxer in contention for a title bout when a blow had left him blind in one eye. During her itinerant Deadhead days, whenever Kat visited her mother and Edith, she and Frank smoked a joint and had athletic sex in the basement, until she realized that he was falling in love with her. She ended the affair before she hurt him. At twenty-one, her life was on the ascent. She was writing free verse and learning the guitar. The Dead's drummer had asked her to dance onstage. She was sailing somewhere remarkable, and Frank was anchored to this neighborhood, still reeling from his injury. That blow had crushed his ambition as much as his sight.

"Hey, Kat!" he shouted from the curb. "You and Edie land somewhere safe?"

"Edie got us a room at the Metropolitan."

"I hear it's a nice hotel. Did you know it used to be a Howard Johnson?"

"I don't think they changed the wallpaper."

"Oh, Kat, you should have seen your place an hour ago. It was crawling with guys in bubble suits."

"Did they fumigate?"

"The guy I talked to said they were just taking samples. You tell Edie I'll keep an eye on her place."

"You're a champ, Frank."

He returned to Gladys's basement for another load.

Ignoring the vacate order, Kat ducked under the police tape and opened their front door, surprised to find it unlocked. She headed straight to Edith's bedroom to get the heart pills. She didn't switch on the lights in case a squad car drove by. She didn't need to. The phosphorescent bloom under Edith's bed gave off enough wattage. She saw the prescription bottle on the nightstand, but she didn't dare move toward it. What looked like iridescent slime was seeping out from under the bed skirt. Muffling her mouth with both hands, she suppressed a scream. Edie had slept in that bed only last night.

She heard footsteps overhead. Vida? Had she snuck back inside too?

Kat marched upstairs and pounded on the door. "Open up, Vida, I know you're there. Edith has been waiting for your call all afternoon." She hammered until the door swung wide.

Sporting a freshly laundered Ziberax T-shirt, Ashley stared at Kat as if she'd knocked on the wrong door, or had come to proselytize.

"Who let you in?" Kat asked.

"Who let you in?" Ashley retorted, the accent syrupy with both old-world irony and new-world sarcasm.

"Where's Vida?"

Ashley shrugged. "I keep place to myself tonight. You call police?"

"You're spending the night? You're not worried about getting sick?"

"No big deal. In Russia, mushrooms grow out people's ears."

"The police told us they were poisonous."

"So don't eat. I fix myself vodka. You want? Vida has Stolichnaya in freezer."

Kat knew she shouldn't, but how could she refuse a stiff drink after what she'd seen downstairs? Besides, she was so curious to see how Vida had refurbished the place. She and Edith had grown up in this building, and Kat remembered their second- and third-floor neighbors—the old Polish lady who used to give them candies to pray for her and Mr. Hernandez, who made Kat and Edith twirl around until he could see their underwear before letting them pass by him on the stoop. Even without lights, Kat saw that all traces of their cluttered lives had been eradicated. The upstairs was now one open space, lined with closets, chic, but impersonal. It dawned on Kat: the second floor was meant to be the master suite as soon as the parlor floor became available: Vida was waiting for Edith to move—or die.

"I come to America to be house sitter, but Vida make me slave," Ashley told Kat, pouring them each a fist-sized shot. "When I refuse to be donkey, she lock me in closet with mushroom."

"Did you tell this to the police?"

"Who believe Russian nobody?"

They sat in the dark kitchen, on stools. Kat intended to have just one, but the fright made her thirsty, and Ashley generously replenished her glass. "You actress like Vida?"

"I've been told more than once that I look like Lauren Bacall, but no, I'm not an actress," Kat said, knowing she should put down her glass and leave. "I'm an author."

"Have I read book by you?"

"You a huge reader?"

Ashley shrugged noncommittally. "I finish *New Earth, Wake Up Life's Purpose.* Maybe next I read you. What book about?"

"It's a collection of my mother's advice columns. She was very famous in her time. She broke all taboos. Have you heard of the G-spot?"

"Yeah, sure thing, G-spot in Russia."

"My mother gave her readers directions for finding it."

"You going to be millionaire!"

"You think so?"

"I know so. You have Russian translator yet? You sell big in Russia."

.   .   .

It was nearly ten p.m. before Kat returned to their hotel room. Edith was sitting up in bed, typing on her BlackBerry.

"Where have you been?" Edith asked.

"Frank said the exterminators took specimens."

"You needed two hours to find that out? Did you go to the pharmacy to get my pills?"

"Oh, *shit.*"

"I'm not supposed to skip a dose."

"I'm sorry. I forgot."

"Is that alcohol I smell?"

"I went inside."

Edith's displeasure softened into slackened awe, just as it had when they were teens and Kat crept through their bedroom window after an all-night date. "What was it like?"

"Oh, Edie, the rug under your bed was glowing. I needed that drink."

After the leathery blonde with the alarmingly big teeth left, Ashley finished the bottle of Stolichnaya, then proceeded to Vida's closet—not the dark cell in which she'd hidden, but the palatial one in the master bedroom. In the week that Ashley had stowed away in Vida's guest room, she'd had more than enough time alone in the apartment to know which of Vida's dresses were a size too big and which looked sexy on her smaller frame.

Dumping out the meager contents of her red suitcase, she began filling it with Vida's dresses, but not before inspecting the closet for mushrooms. She knew what happened to those aged Russians with mushrooms growing out of their ears: they coughed up black blood and died.

She had grown up with eight siblings in a Soviet-era apartment complex outside Omsk. Girls like her got called *insignificuntskis*. One of two futures awaited her: married with babies, or unmarried with babies. Ashley hated babies. Her mother and father were speechless when she announced that she'd signed up with a nanny agency. The "Au Pair in America" brochure had promised that "the time of your life starts here, you will experience American culture, improve your English, gain self-confidence, make new friends, and have fun. *Au pair* means *on par,* which is exactly what you will be—an equal member of your host family."

She was eighteen. She'd never been on an airplane before. As a going-away present, her parents gave her a cardboard suitcase that she painted red. Her host family, a divorced theater agent and a goatish male toddler, treated her anything but *on par*. The divorcée, a hysterical hen with only one chick, constantly pecked at Ashley for the slightest infractions, while the toddler, Zachary, would butt her with his thick skull whenever she tried to pick him up. The hard bones felt like budding horns were about to sprout.

In the three weeks she'd slept in a tiny maid's room off the hen's kitchen, she gained no self-confidence, made no new friends, and had no fun, though her English did improve. The hen ran her agency from the basement suite of her Village brownstone. Ashley didn't get to meet any of her boss's famous clients, though she sometimes heard affected theatrical laughter through the air vents. Photographs of the agency's stable adorned the stairwell leading up from the street—actors in profile, laughing, posing solemnly, kissing passionately, a fat man wearing a judge's robes, the actress from the Ziberax commercial garbed as a queen. The first time Ashley watched the commercial on the hen's television, she hadn't been able to guess what was being sold. She'd been too distracted by the actress, who appeared to have it all—beauty and money and minions—yet still pouted. Only later did Ashley realize that the queen in the photograph and the spoiled lady in the commercial were one and the same.

During her short employment, as soon as the hen would leave for one of her lengthy lunches, Ashley would abandon Zachary shrieking in his crib and go downstairs to snoop around the office and leaf through the Rolodex and booking datebook. That's how Ashley learned where Vida lived and when she was supposed to be out of town doing a play.

On Ashley's last morning of employment, before the hysterical Americunt threw her out on the street, she finished copying down all the names and addresses in the Rolodex and datebook, though how that information would serve her was still a mystery. Blotched with fury, the hen had dragged her across the living room, sat her in front of the television, inserted a DVD, and played a movie starring Ashley, the American name Anna Alevtina Sokolov had picked out for herself—Ashley muting the shrieking baby monitor; Ashley giving Zachary a tiny chip of Ambien to help him nap; Ashley going downstairs to root around the hen's office.

She'd been given five minutes to pack and get out. She hauled her red suitcase to Vida's address. According to the datebook, Vida was supposed to be out of town for the next two weeks. Ashley had been trying to figure out how to break in when the leathery blonde had mistaken her for Vida's maid and unlocked the garden door for her.

Ashley selected one last outfit from Vida's closet and laid it carefully atop the hillock of finery already piled in her red suitcase. She had to wonder how she had let herself be caught twice in a row by security cameras, though she was certain no one was watching her tonight. What kind of country was this where private citizens hide cameras in toys and pencil sharpeners? Even in Putin's Russia, people didn't do that.

Her favorite place in Vida's apartment wasn't the living room, or the cedar-paneled steam room, or the master bedroom with the memory-foam mattress and the forty-seven-inch flat-screen television. Ashley preferred a harder bed. No, her favorite room was the office: smoky glass desk, leather chair, the walls displaying Vida's accomplishments—framed awards and a photo array of her various roles. The pictures weren't particularly flattering. The photographs hadn't been chosen out of petty vanity, but from regal self-possession, and Ashley intended to learn those poses, even if she had to fake it. She'd always been a sloucher, but not anymore.

Her plan was to try the next available apartment in the hen's datebook, an actor away in London for the month. Her only other option was to phone her parents collect and ask them to call all the relatives to see if anyone could loan her money to get home. Who would loan her money? No one in the family spoke to her except her uncle, and he didn't have two rubles to rub together. Ashley had cased the actor's apartment after the police had let her go, a glass tower on the East River only ten blocks away. She'd introduced herself to the doorman, a big-eared boy built like a draft horse, and told him that she was the actor's house sitter and would be moving in tomorrow. She planned to spend one last night at Vida's and sleep in the master bedroom, not in the guest closet with the mushrooms.

The first time she'd hidden in that small dark space after Vida had arrived home unexpectedly, the sensory deprava-tion had come as a relief. No more having to affect bravery when all she felt was fear. She spent the first hour of her confinement eating chocolates from Vida's stash, the only sound her lips sucking contentedly on the sugar. But when the chocolates were finished and she opened her eyes, all she saw was blackness. She reached to either side of her prone body: walls. The closet had been the length and breadth of a coffin. She panicked that she would suffocate alone in her dark grave. She went through her pockets and found a book of matches. Lighting one, she stared up at Vida's hanging coats and dresses. The colors, so vibrant after the blackness, buoyed her spirits. Only when the flame singed her fingertips did she blow it out. By touch, she counted six more matches. Though she had always thought her mother a superstitious peasant, it had been her mother's fire incantations that Anushka Sokolov had whispered in the dark. The next time she lit a match, she made an offering. She promised the flame everything she had in her red suitcase if only it wouldn't go out. But out it went. She lit another and swore to the flame that she'd go back to Omsk, get married, and have babies, but the flame didn't believe her. It hurried down the stick and burnt her fingers again. Finally, there were no more matches and nothing left to bargain with but her soul. That's when she'd seen the ethereal glow emanating from the closet corner. She hadn't been buried alive after all.

When Vida stepped onto the stage it wasn't to bask in attention, it was to disappear.

To submit to another's will and permit an alien soul to inhabit her body and control her expressions—all fifty-six facial muscles, and the coloration of her skin, and the tempo of her breathing, and her hair and teeth and cartilage and bones—was the deepest intimacy Vida knew. Acting gave her the only moments of respite she had from herself.

She had wanted to perform ever since she could remember, even after other children made it perfectly clear that her drama wasn't necessarily playing in their heads. She spent hours at her mother's vanity mirror, with its makeup pots and eyelash curler, reenacting scenes from television shows. By chance, she discovered that with a slight tensing of her forehead, she could make herself look Filipina like her mother, and with a loosening of that same brow appear Black Irish like her father. In high school, the assistant drama coach tried to discourage her from auditioning for Juliet by telling her that Asian faces were too enigmatic for the stage. She not only got the part, she won her first standing ovation. She arrived in Manhattan from Amityville, Long Island, in the early nineties, twenty years old, along with tens of thousands of other aspiring actors. She studied everything from classical voice training to Stanislavski, but the best book she ever read on the subject was Darwin's *The Expression of the Emotions in Man and Animals.* A teacher, an older man who had come to acting from stand-up comedy, had assigned it to her when she had been unable to relax during an improvisational skit. "Assuming the expression," he had told her, "doesn't just buy you time, it frees you." Page after page, with objectivity and sly wit, Darwin deconstructed every possible configuration that a face might assume, every permutation of a smile, frown, wince, sneer, tick, and snarl, be it man's or beast's. The first time she had practiced an expression in front of the mirror as rigorously as Darwin had described it, it finally sank in—acting wasn't about what you felt, it was about what you conveyed.

Take Darwin's description of "horror."

> The raising of the eyebrows is necessary so the eyes open quickly and widely; this movement produces transverse wrinkles across the forehead. The degree to which the eyes and mouth are opened corresponds with the degree of horror felt; but these movements must be coordinated—a widely opened mouth with only slightly raised eyebrows results in a meaningless grimace.

Though outwardly Vida's facial expression remained calm (she watched herself in the Manhattan-bound taxi's rearview mirror), she could feel her eyebrows straining to rise, her eyes aching to pop open, whenever she thought of the mushroom. After checking into the Lohito Grand and taking a long, hot, necessary shower, she phoned her insurance company to find out what, exactly, her mold coverage was. During the hellish wait for a human voice, she caught her expression in one of the hotel room's many mirrors. It was what Darwin described as "defiance"—a slight uncovering of the canine tooth on one side of the face. When a voice finally answered, she read off her policy number, longer than the national debt.

"Am I covered for mold?" Vida asked.

"Do you have a mold rider?"

"I have whatever you sold me."

Vida heard nails clicking on keys.

"Your area is in an orange zone, no mold riders."

"I must have some kind of mold coverage. I pay over eight thousand a year."

"Do you have water damage?"

"My super says no."

Again, the sharp clicking nails.

"What kind of mold is it?"

"The fire chief didn't know."

"The HAZMAT squad was called?"

Click, click, click, click.

"You'll need to phone this number. It's our mold rider division."

"I thought you said I was in the orange zone."

She didn't call the mold division; she called Virginia, her manager and oldest friend in New York. They'd been roommates in their early twenties, splitting a railroad apartment over a booming gay bar in Alphabet City. They had painted the living room black. Vida had been Virginia's first client, when Virginia defied her starchy judge father by not joining his old law practice and opening a theatrical agency instead. Lately, though, Vida heard mounting exasperation in Virginia's tone whenever Vida demanded to know why Virginia wasn't sending her out on auditions. Virginia had cautioned her as an agent *and* a friend that if Vida became the face of Ziberax she could damage her stage career. ("Desdemona on Ziberax might change the meaning of the play, don't you think?") But the renovations were costing a fortune, and Vida was tired of being poor.

After extracting a promise from Virginia that she'd call Vida's insurance company and use her threatening lawyer-speak to find out what, exactly, was going to be covered, Vida poured herself a minibar Scotch and phoned her mother in the Philippines. Her mother had moved back to Lapu-Lapu City six years ago, after her father died. The sun would just be rising over the Cebu Sea. It was already tomorrow there.

When her mother answered, all Vida's theatrics fell away, even her greatest role, the self-confident Vida, and she once again became wide-eyed, gap-mouthed Debbi.

She heard the news on an early-morning talk show while pouring herself a cup of room-service coffee: the actress playing Goneril in tonight's *King Lear* at Shakespeare in the Park had fainted during yesterday's steam-bath outdoor dress rehearsal and knocked out her front teeth. Vida immediately phoned the director, an old friend, to plead her case. She had just played Goneril last year with the ensemble, at the Stratford Festival, under his direction. It was exactly the sort of role that Vida was meant to play, and the director knew it. Why would he compromise with a mediocre understudy? The oldest daughter of King Lear, and one of Shakespeare's most odious ladies, Goneril doesn't especially have many memorable lines. How could she? She speaks only lies. Any actress who plays her must arrest the attention of the back row by her facial reactions to what others say in her presence, how she looks when her father says to her, "How sharper than a serpent's tooth it is to have a thankless child!" The director, with whom she'd had a tender but passionless affair, told her to come by at ten but promised nothing. During the initial casting, the producer had objected to Vida because of that asinine commercial.

Outside the Public Theater, a short walk from her hotel, Vida was about to turn off her cell when it vibrated. Virginia's name appeared in the window. She let the phone shiver in her hand. She couldn't risk becoming too distracted before the audition, though the director had assured her that a reading wasn't necessary, just a friendly chat with the producer. But not answering her phone proved even more distracting. "Am I covered?" she asked before Virginia's call went to voicemail.

"The insurance agent assigned to your case is a snake," Virginia said. "He wouldn't give me a straight answer. In any case, nothing can be done or decided until the test results are in. Their people need to determine which kind of mold you have. Apparently, there are a million varieties. You can have your own experts examine the samples as well. Here's the rub: some molds are covered by your policy while others are considered 'acts of God,' which essentially means your insurance company will refuse to pay."

"How can they refuse? Aren't all molds acts of God if you believe in Him, or not if you don't? When did State Farm become religious?" asked Vida, trying to restrain her ire so that it didn't taint the audition, though ire wouldn't be such a ruinous thing to feel when reading for Goneril.

"Meantime, get your super to look around the basement for leaky pipes. If there's a leak, it's man-made, and that's good. If there's no leak, find out if your neighbors have mushrooms."

There were still ten minutes before the audition. Normally, Vida would spend this lost time—what she called the waiting room of the imagination—walking around the block with great measure as if she were following her character, miming the way a queen might pull back her shoulders and tilt up her chin until her carriage looked puffed up with pride. But today, she called Frank instead.

"Frank, are there any leaks in the basement I don't know about?"

"Place was dry last time I took out the garbage," he said.

"Could you ask the neighbors if anyone else has mold, if anyone's seen any mushrooms? They're easy to spot. They glow in the dark."

"I haven't heard nothing about no glow, but Gladys found a mushroom growing out of her shower drain."

"Where does Gladys live?"

"Right next door to you. She's the lady with the cat hotel. She's not admitting it now. Why would she? She don't want to get kicked out of her house like you. Want to know what I think?" He didn't wait for her answer. "It's some kind of killer mold from when Hurricane Sandy mixed up with that old oil spill. It's not just me thinking that either. It was on the internet."

"What are you talking about?"

"The Greenpoint oil spill, it was bigger than *Valdez*. Until the Gulf it was our biggest ever. It's been leaking since 1940. Whenever the telephone company digs a hole for a pole, they strike oil."

"I have to go, Frank, I have an audition."

"What's the part? You should make a movie about your life and call it Andromeda Strain II."

Vida sat down before the director, a very thin, concave-chested man (no wonder the affair had been passionless), and the producer, a short man just shy of being a midget. The producer gave her the *grin*. She'd heard he was sleeping with the understudy.

Before either man could speak, Vida announced she would read from act one, Goneril's groveling reply to the King's petulant, vain question. The director fed her the cue lines: "Which of you shall we say doth love us most? . . . Goneril, our eldest born, speak first."

> Sir, I love you more than words can wield the matter;
> Dearer than eyesight, space, and liberty;
> Beyond what can be valued, rich or rare;
> No less than life; with grace, health, beauty, honor;
> As much as child e'er lov'd, or father found;
> A love that makes breath poor and speech unable . . .

Vida paused. This pause was the make-or-break moment for any actress playing Goneril. In less than ten heartbeats, ruthlessness, wile, avarice, and betrayal must be conveyed in halted silence. But Vida wasn't using the ten heartbeats to think about Goneril's inheritance, she was thinking about the glowing mushrooms infesting her beloved home. Vida sensed her jaw muscles going slack and her eyes begin to open wide in horror. But the professional in her took charge, and only a rumble of fear crossed her features, intensifying the expression she was trying to achieve—icy calculation over molten treachery. When she spoke again, her tone was pure adoration and fidelity.

Beyond all manner of so much I love you.

She'd wiped that grin right off the producer's face.

"Okay?" the director asked him.

He nodded in awed, capitulating silence.

Later, as she left the theater heady from the victory and still immersed in her performance, halfway between pre-Roman Britain and twenty-first-century Manhattan, she didn't notice the opening salvos of a storm, or that the western sky was solid with purple and black thunderheads. Only when a cool wind stood her arm hairs on end was she aware that the temperature had dropped by degrees after three weeks of gelatinous humidity. The heavens were favoring her! What was Edmund's line? *Fools by heavenly compulsion.* Minutes later, when the sky opened up and assaulted her with rubber-hard pellets of rain, she reveled in the beating.

"When God came to Noah and told him a great flood would come and cover the earth, Noah had forewarning according to tort law," Edith used to tell the second-year law interns as she toured them around Price, Bloodworth's library. "Did Noah take any actions to prevent the flood?" she would query their blank faces. "He never prayed for the wicked as Abraham did. He never warned his neighbors or business partners that if they didn't amend their immoral, depraved conduct a deluge was imminent. He took no precautions to ensure the welfare of anyone else but himself and his own and his animals. Tort law is the calculus of negligence."

She knew the interns didn't really understand what a legal librarian did. They imagined it entailed filing away books after the lawyers were finished. They assumed the job required great organization but little imagination. To the contrary. The law wasn't about ethics: it was about precedent and research. No lawyer billing six hundred an hour had the time or the inclination to truly grasp, as a good legal librarian did, the case-by-case, ruling-by-ruling, statute-by-statute, tome-by-tome law, which was, in Edith's opinion, the very marrow of justice. To find precedent in that vast archive required something akin to inspiration. Edith would have a hunch and then unearth the facts until a precedent was exposed.

Here were the facts in the case she was building against Vida: Vida had been notified seven days previously about a foul odor and potential mold problem in the basement. Edith had left five additional voicemails in as many days notifying Vida about the dangerous infestation. She had also slipped a written complaint under Vida's door, and mailed a certified copy of that letter, though she had no idea where it would be delivered now that the building had been condemned.

She was anxious about the archive. Each of the hundred-thousand-plus letters would need to be individually tested for spores, fumigated, and then retested. She could hardly ship them to the Smithsonian otherwise, risk infecting the National Archives. And could the oldest, most friable letters withstand whatever chemical bath they would be subjected to? How much would that cost?

She finally reached Vida the next morning. Vida must have been caught off guard, because Edith's call didn't transfer to voicemail like it had the previous ten times. Edith noted the hour: eleven sharp. She was keeping a log of her calls. She'd just gotten off the phone after seeking counsel from Stanley Flom, senior partner at Price, Bloodworth, the husband of Alice, Edith's secret lover for twenty-two years.

"How dare you ignore my calls!" Edith's voice detonated in pent-up rage when Vida answered. "My mother's archives are being infested every minute you delay!"

"I know, I know. Can we talk a little later?" Vida said. "It's pouring out and I didn't bring an umbrella."

Edith glanced out the hotel window for the first time that morning. The sky was swollen and violet, the expressway ablaze with headlights, but the streets looked dry.

"It's not raining here. Don't you dare hang up on me, Vida. I need to know what's going on and when we can safely go back. My mother's archive is due at the Smithsonian by the end of next month. We'll need to hire an archival conservator to work with the fumigators. What is your insurance policy going to cover?"

"The only thing I know for certain," Vida shouted over the rumble of thunder, "is that my insurance company is trying to claim it's an act of God and is threatening not to cover anything."

The line went dead.

Edith didn't believe for a second that a crack of lightning had interrupted the signal. Why would Vida employ that arcane term? *Act of God.* It was rarely used nowadays. It confused jurors, who might be awestruck by the concept of divine manifestation. "Act of Nature" was the popular term, though "act of God" remained the legal one. Vida must have already spoken to a real estate attorney, one with a savvy librarian, otherwise how would she have known that only an act of God could void their mother's rent-controlled lease? Vida clearly intended to turn this temporary eviction into a permanent one.

After the disturbing call, Edith went to the window. Fistfuls of rain were now being thrown against the glass. She could no longer see the expressway, only red taillights, bleeding pinpricks in the downpour. Kat was out there somewhere. She'd slipped out while Edith was on the phone with Stanley. She'd taken the manuscript with her, the only letters Edith could be certain were safe, and now it was pouring out. She'd probably forgotten to take an umbrella.

Edith had nursed their mother during her protracted, pitiless illness with little assistance from Kat, except for the occasional, erratic visit from the West Coast, the airfare always paid for by Edith. She had tried to convince their mother to put Kat's share of the inheritance, modest after the medical bills, into a trust that wouldn't begin until Kat turned sixty-five, but their mother fell into a coma and then she died, and Kat had gone through her share in less than two years, saving nothing for old age.

Fatigue settled over Edith like a mist, yet her pulse thumped wildly as if she'd just had a fright. Along the periphery of her vision, she noticed the familiar scintillation that invariably heralded a migraine. She'd forgotten to pack her headache pills, too. Where was Kat when she needed her? She had no choice but to lie down, though the Housing Department still needed to be called to get a copy of their mother's lease now that the original had been eaten. When the first volley of pain struck just behind her right temple, she tried to shield her eyes from the blinding explosion, but her left arm was missing. Had it been blown off in the blast? She saw it on the bed beside her. She tried to lift it. It might as well have been an I-beam. The next piercing barrage left her skull ringing. When she came to, she was safely back in Price, Bloodworth's silent library. She should look up "act of God." She rolled the stepladder over to the wall bricked with New York tort law volumes, and pulled down the relevant tome. She sat at her desk and opened it, but to her surprise and escalating fear, all six hundred and seven pages were blank. On the far side of the library, Kat burst noisily through the mahogany doors, and once again, Edith felt that amalgamation of dread and monolithic love that she always experienced whenever she saw Kat.

"Edie, oh, Edie!" Kat shouted hoarsely, then froze. "Are you dead?"

"Quiet! You're in a library."

Shielding the manuscript from the sudden downpour, Kat bolted across Fifth Avenue. She didn't have an actual appointment with the editor from Sutton House, though when they had spoken on the phone two months earlier, he had told her that his mother had been a huge fan of Dr. Mimi's column; he could still remember her reading the choicest letters aloud to his father at breakfast. He promised to look at the collection as soon as Kat culled the archive down to the hundred best, impossible a task as that might be.

She had only planned to drop off the letters with his secretary this morning, and was surprised and grateful when the editor himself came out of his office to greet her, an unexpectedly thin man twig-necked like a heron.

"You look just like the newspaper picture of Dr. Mimi that I remember," he told Kat.

He seemed so friendly and affable, Kat wondered if they wouldn't sign the contract today. She wanted badly to bring Edith some good news. She had no idea what Sutton House would pay, but whatever it was, she'd finally be contributing. Even before the evacuation, Edith had worried about money. Kat couldn't begin to guess what a librarian might have been able to save for old age, but it couldn't be much, despite Edith's lifetime of frugality. Even as a little girl, she'd squirreled away her weekly candy allotment while Kat gobbled up hers, and then, when Kat ached for sugar, Edith would sell her M&M's at a nickel apiece. As far as Kat knew, besides the four years at Skidmore, her sister had never left home. The summer they turned twenty-one, Kat begged Edith to join her at Woodstock, take acid, and dance naked under the stars. Kat honestly believed that if Edith had just one out-of-body experience, she'd at least have a choice whether to abide by the laws of this unjust world or chase after ethereal gusts of grandeur, as Kat planned to do. Instead, Edith had taken a summer internship in Price, Bloodworth's library and fixed her fate. By thirty, she was stout and middle-aged. Why would she scrimp and deny herself during youth, with all its electric pleasures and titillating temptations, so she could eat well in old age? What? Salisbury steak? The astringent life Edith subjected herself to pained Kat.

Sitting across from the editor in his cramped, messy office, Kat watched his agreeable face frown as she handed him the manuscript. She had kept all the contenders in a three-ring binder, each letter sheathed in its own plastic sleeve. Some of the letters were more than fifty years old. The paper ranged from the back of a Chock full o' Nuts place mat to a wedding napkin. More than one had been penned on toilet paper. Kat believed that the handwriting said as much as the words. The grieving wrote so lightly, it almost looked as if they wished to disappear too. The infatuated scribbled away in loopy exuberance. She was still hoping to persuade the editor to reproduce the original letters as photographs, not just plain text.

He weighed the manuscript in his hands as if it were a brick of pig iron. "You do realize we publish novelty books, not encyclopedias."

Opening the binder, he flipped through the three-hundred-plus pages. Kat noted a look of discomfort sweep across his affable expression. "I'm sure each one of these letters deserves to be included, but we agreed to keep the number under a hundred. And this one is in pencil. I can barely read it. Where's the typescript with your mother's replies?"

Kat had invested so much in this book that the heroic effort it took to maintain her composure faltered. She could no longer blink back the tears.

The editor found her some tissues. He kept a stash handy in his top drawer. Kat couldn't help but wonder how many of his writers he made cry.

"I don't usually behave like this, but you can't imagine what the last two days have been like," Kat said, taking a Kleenex and blotting her eyes. When she lowered the tissue, she could see him staring at the slightly ajar door like a castaway fixes on the horizon in hope of a rescue ship. She took charge of herself. It was her moment to chase after a gust of grandeur. She reached across his desk and opened the binder to the penciled letter he'd dismissed. "It's *supposed* to be difficult to read, that's the point. Look at the signature: 'Bereft in Plattsburg.' It's the mark of grief."

But he didn't look down at bereavement's fingerprint. He remained focused on the exit.

"These letters are an oral history, a public diary. And they're not just words, they're artifacts," Kat said, keeping her tone impassioned but subdued to hide her tears. "Seeing how a hand carves out meaning with a pencil point lets us remember that the human touch is essential." She closed the binder and placed her hand on it, as if she were about to swear on something sacred. "Please, all I ask is that you read these letters with an open mind."

He did not say no.

. . .

When Kat got outside, the storm was raging. She dreaded facing Edith without the salve of good news. She darted into the first refuge she found, an old-fashioned Midtown bar—garnet-red stools, a sticky counter, and an ancient bartender whose wooden face told nothing. She shook her head, like a dog does, to fling off the water. The only other patron, a slight middle-aged man with hairy wrists, was dry. He must have already started drinking well before the storm. Why not be friendly and sit beside him?

"I usually don't have a cocktail before noon, but I've come from my publisher and I could do with a drink. Stoli," she called to the bartender, wondering how she would pay for both it and Edith's prescription, which she intended to pick up before returning to the hotel. She had less than twenty dollars in her purse. She might as well go for broke. "Make that a double, please."

An electric storm the likes of which Ashley had never seen before drenched her within seconds, but she couldn't walk any faster hauling her heavy red suitcase stuffed to bursting with Vida's finery. By the time she reached the glass tower on the river, her suitcase's seams had come unglued and the red color, which she had painted over the ugly gray cardboard with exhilarating anticipation of her upcoming adventure in America, now dripped what looked like a trail of blood. The doorman from yesterday ran outside with an umbrella and offered to carry the bleeding suitcase, but she shook her head. It was all she owned. In the lobby, it nearly fell apart in her hands. She opened the latches. Just as she feared, everything was wet and ruined. A sorrow she suspected had little to do with the stained plunder surprised her, and a hiccupping sob escaped before the tears came.

"Hey, hey, don't cry," said the doorman. "We'll put everything in Mr. Sam's washing machine."

"I lock myself out."

He kindly offered to use his master key, and then carried her bloated bag for her, holding it together as best he could. In the elevator, he snuck a glance at her breasts when he thought she wasn't looking. Her sopping wet T-shirt was nearly transparent. The ZIBERAX lettered across her chest looked as if it had been tattooed on her naked breasts.

"You'll need to press the button," he said after the doors closed and they didn't ascend. His hands were occupied trying to keep her suitcase from bleeding on his shoes.

But Ashley didn't know which floor the actor lived on. She pressed all thirty buttons.

"In Russia, you press all or you go nowhere."

Outside the actor's apartment on the second floor, the doorman set down her now shapeless suitcase on the welcome mat, which quickly turned red, before opening the door with his master key.

"Thank you, you very kind to poor Russia girl locked out in storm," Ashley said.

"You an actress too?" he asked, after he set her worldly possessions on the actor's wooden floor. A red lake instantly formed.

"I new Ziberax girl. Big secret. Don't tell."

Alone in the apartment, she filled the tub with hot water and laundry soap she found under the sink. She didn't know how to use the washing machine. She couldn't save the whites—they were now pink, like bubble gum—but she was able to rescue a black silk dress and designer jeans, any fabric or color where a tint of red wouldn't be noticed. She hung them over the tub to dry, and then washed what was left of her worldly things—her hairbrush was now saturated in red, like a paintbrush, and her emery board looked like a bloody dagger. Around the suitcase, the red lake was rising. She considered the mess and shrugged in humble resignation, just as her mother had shrugged whenever she had looked at the mess of her daughter Anushka. She walked over to the big window facing the skyline. Lightning appeared to spark from turret to spike. Wet, windy slaps buffeted the glass. The normally sluggish black river had whitecaps. She'd never before seen weather as drama. In Omsk, the weather snuck up on you like an invisible gas: one instant you could breathe, the next frigid air scalded your lungs; one second you could see across the street, the next you were blinded by snow.

She heard knocking at the door and peeked through the eyehole's wide-angle lens. The doorman's ears appeared even bigger than usual.

"I brought you a clean doormat from the penthouse," he said, rolling up the stained one and then rolling out the new one.

"You telling me penthouse owner say, yeah, sure thing, just take my mat?"

"No one lives there. It's the model apartment."

She'd never before heard the term "model apartment," and it evoked a thrilling perfection, the apartment to which all other apartments aspire.

"It has an awesome view," he stammered, shuffling his heavy feet in place. "Want to see it?"

The penthouse's living room was as big as the shoe factory her parents slaved in. The ceiling was as tall as a telephone pole. Three out of four walls were glass. From the vantage point of the thirtieth floor, the tempest's production became grander. Behind the skyline, banks and banks of clouds waited to come onstage.

She turned her attention to the furniture. The dining room table was set for six as if in preparation for a dinner party. The beds were made. The office desk had an open laptop, lit with icons. She touched the keys. They didn't give. The computer was only a hollow plastic shell painted to look like a laptop. Did Americans decorate their homes with plastic electronics like her mother tried to beautify their hovel with plastic fruit? She wished her mother could see her eldest daughter now, but even if her mother had miraculously appeared, she wouldn't have been impressed. To be impressed, you needed to want, and her mother appeared to want nothing. On wintery Sunday afternoons, after the family, except Anushka, returned from church, her mother would settle half asleep in the dark living room, her mind as empty as her pockets. And if Ashley had blinked and her father had miraculously appeared, he would probably have groveled to the doorman just because he was in uniform. Her father had spent ten years in a gulag. He was used to living in holes. He'd look around and then cower at being so exposed to the elements, like a mouse in an open field.

"I'm not supposed to let anyone up here. We should probably leave," said the doorman as Ashley started to make herself comfortable on the sofa.

She patted the cushion beside her. "Come. Sit by me."

"I could get fired if one of the real estate agents comes by for a showing."

She'd sized him up correctly yesterday—a gelded draft horse that thinks he's a stallion.

Back in the actor's apartment, she hunted for food. She hadn't eaten since yesterday morning. It must be lunchtime, though the black clouds made it look like midnight. She opened the refrigerator. Unlike Vida's shelves, which held only a small ration of wilted vegetables and queen-sized chocolate bars, this actor's fridge was stocked for a siege. She began to inspect the jars, bottles, boxes, and fruits only an oligarch could afford in Russia. She wanted to taste everything—pineapple (better than rock candy), Finocchiona salami (a fatty hard old sausage), Dean & Deluca Single Origin Truffles (tastier than Vida's chocolates), Bella Viva dried fruit (she could buy the same kind in the Omsk marketplace), Dean & Deluca Mesquite and Stout Ale Mustard (she ate a spoonful), East Shore Dipping Pretzels (not

salty enough), Lambrusco Wine Jelly (too much like medicine), hickory-smoked almonds (she finished the jar), but-
ter caramels, olive oil, Grissini Breadsticks, and a carton of
Yunnan organic green tea ice cream (it didn't taste like tea
at all).

She felt sick but didn't stop. She gorged as the storm
raged outside.

Kat didn't get back to the hotel until well past midnight. Lenny, the hairy-wristed gentleman from the bar, had paid for her drinks. At some point during the afternoon, they'd staggered back to Lenny's place, a walk-up in Hell's Kitchen. He was almost a head shorter than Kat, but Kat believed that horizontally everyone was the same height. His hairy wrists were just the beginning of his pelt. For someone steeped in an afternoon of alcohol, Lenny was an attentive, hopeful lover, and Kat couldn't help but think, what better way to spend a rainy day than two strangers comforting each other? She might have fooled the world with her hearty sexuality, but she never could fool herself. She was lonely.

She quietly shut the hotel door so as not to wake Edith. She didn't want a lecture on how irresponsible she was not phoning to let Edith know she was alive. Thank god she'd remembered to stop by the twenty-four-hour pharmacy to pick up Edith's heart pills. She placed the vial on Edith's side of their shared nightstand so her pills would be the first thing Edith saw when she woke up, in case Kat had to sleep in to ward off a hangover. She already tasted the chalky dehydration that promised a headache. In the dark, she shed her wet clothes, slipped under the sheets, and then pulled up the blanket. It was surprisingly chilly, though whether from air-conditioning or the storm, Kat wasn't sure. Her pupils drank in what little ambient streetlight there was. She watched Edith materialize out of the gloom. Edith had fallen asleep on top of her blanket, in her bra and underwear. She didn't want Edith to freeze, but unearthing the blanket from under her would only wake her. Kat stripped off her own blanket and covered Edith, then got back under the cold sheets.

She closed her eyes, anticipating the comforting wholeness that twins share when they sleep near each other. She had once attended an identical-twins conference, without Edith, and had met others who experienced what she had. Twins have been known to send each other messages in dreams, even when they're sleeping in different hemispheres, though Edith didn't believe any of that. Whether she believed or not, she was always waiting for Kat in sleep's antechamber, though Edith took different spirit and animal forms. No matter where in the world Kat was, when she closed her eyes for the night, Edith's presence came to her, like a scent, and Kat believed that she visited Edith nightly in exactly the same way. Tonight, however, all she could smell was Lenny on her.

Maybe Edith was only pretending to be asleep?

"Edie, are you awake?" she whispered.

She listened for a response, but heard nothing. Sleepers' exhalations were always discernable: silence was the lie. "Edie, don't be mad at me. I got your pills. They're on the nightstand."

Again, nothing. Was she so angry that she wouldn't speak to Kat?

"What do you want from me, Edie? I can't live like a nun. I'm not like you. I can't suffer loneliness with your stoicism. Is that such a horrible, unforgivable need that you feel you have to shun me?"

Kat switched on the light. Edith's eyes were open, but she wasn't looking at her. Kat rose. "Edie?" She stared straight into those pale blue irises. The forest-green coronas looked moist and alive, but the pupils were opaque. Nobody was looking back at Kat. She lowered her ear against Edith's chest to listen for life but flinched when the skin felt cold. Kat's heart banged so loudly she couldn't distinguish any pulse but her own. She thought she'd heard a faint echo from deep within Edith.

She dialed 911. "My sister isn't breathing. I can't find her pulse. Help us. Please, help us."

After dispatching the paramedics, the operator asked, "Could she be choking on anything?"

Kat knew that Edith wasn't choking, but the operator's commands filled her with purpose.

"Make sure her airway is clear. Are there any signs of trauma?"

Should she close her sister's lids? Edith was such a private woman. She wouldn't want strangers to see her soulless eyes. Closing Edith's eyelids was the most heartrending sensation that Kat had ever experienced. The once blinking, widening, animated lids obediently shut.

The pandemonium of paramedics stilled only after it became evident that Edith wouldn't be shocked back to life. The two men, older than Kat imagined medics to be, must have seen their share of weeping wives, howling husbands, and sobbing parents—but not twins. They were momentarily taken aback when they saw that the corpse and the bereft were identical.

"Can I ride with her to the hospital?" Kat asked as they were fitting Edith into a body bag.

The two men exchanged alarmed glances. "We're not taking her to the hospital."

That was when it finally sank in. Edith was going to the morgue.

"Do you want a moment to say good-bye?" asked the taller man before closing the bag.

"We've already said good-bye."

Edith was then zipped up, strapped on the gurney, and trundled away. Kat accompanied her as far as the elevator.

"Is there someone you can call to be with you tonight?" asked the shorter man.

The elevator door closed before Kat could answer him.

She returned to their hotel room, though that was the last place she wanted to go and lie down. A horror she'd never before known began to occupy the empty bed beside her. She thought she smelled death on the sheets. How long had Edith been dead? Oh god, let death have come quick; let her not have suffered long and alone. The odor—almost sweet—was still there. Kat stripped Edith's bed, and left the sheets balled in the corridor for the maid. That's when the messy, gulping sobs began, liquid grief. When she finally came up for air, she called the front desk.

"My sister just died. Is the bar closed?"

The Indian-accented young man stammered an enigmatic "I'm sorry, ma'am."

"Sorry the bar is closed or sorry my sister is dead?"

"Both," he said.

A few minutes later, he knocked on the door with an open bottle of Scotch.

"A guest left this behind," he explained.

"Would you like to stay for a drink?" asked Kat. She couldn't bear to be alone.

"Nobody's watching the front desk."

"Please. Just one."

"I could lose my job."

She let the poor man leave, but still poured two glasses, one for herself, and one for Edith. The loneliness felt both cavernous and suffocating. Edith had been alone and without her pills. Why hadn't Kat gone straight to the pharmacy? Why did she have to go home with Lenny? Why did she have to get drunk with Ashley? She was such a fuckup and now her sister was dead.

Daylight brought no comfort, though Kat had spent every waking hour of the night yearning for dawn. When she managed to doze off and forget that Edith was dead, the naked mattress was there to remind her when she opened her eyes. Why had she stripped the bed? She went into the hall to find the sheets, but the bundle was gone.

The Scotch bottle was nearly empty. She picked up Edith's vial of heart pills. The label warned of sleepiness. She took three with the last swig. Between the booze and the beta-blockers, she finally sank into slumber, where she found herself dining with Edith in an Egyptian restaurant she didn't recognize. Edith was relishing her food, a cut of rare lamb that she ate off the bone.

Kat waited until Edith finished before telling her the awful news. "Edie," she said hoarsely. "Oh, Edie, I'm so sorry to tell you this, but you have to know. You're dead."

"I just finished eating my dinner. I'm no more dead than you."

Two mustachioed waiters came over. One grabbed Edith's wrists, the other her ankles, and swing-tossed her off the balcony, a ten-story fall to her death.

Kat finished her dinner, so grateful that the kind waiters had taken things into their own hands and spared Edith any more suffering. But when her plate was empty, she began to fret that Edith might not have died instantly, that she might have hit the pavement, crushed and in agony. Kat ran down endless flights of stairs. When she reached the street, Edith was sitting on the curb, stunned and shaken by the ten-story fall, but unharmed.

Kat burst into tears of elation. "I thought I'd never see you alive again!"

She woke momentarily euphoric, but then the naked mattress stripped her of that illusion.

She waited until a decent hour, nine sharp, before tolling the death bell. She called Edith's old friends from work. She found their numbers in the BlackBerry.

"Hello, Janice."

"You sound awful, Edie."

"It's Kat. Edith is dead."

"Oh, no. No, no, no. How? When?"

"Last night. I found her. I don't even know where they took the body. I forgot to ask."

"Call Stanley. He's Edie's executor. I can't believe she's gone."

"Neither can I," said Kat.

She wasn't ready to call Edith's executor. The word sounded too final. She took another beta-blocker to buffet her thumping anxiety. What if Edith had taken her medicine that morning? What if Kat weren't such a fuckup? Would Edith be alive? Did she call anyone for help at the last minute?

Kat reached for the BlackBerry. It contained so much of Edith's life it seemed like a sacred memory totem. Edith's last call was to Vida, probably the last person Edith spoke to. It was placed at eleven a.m. sharp and lasted two minutes and nineteen seconds. What had they talked about? Did Vida say something that gave her a heart attack? The call before that was to Stanley. Did he say something that killed her? Who was the last person she emailed? Edith's AOL account asked for a password. I'm her twin, Kat thought, we shared every cell in our bodies for sixty-four years, surely I can guess her password. The account locked after ten failed attempts, and then Kat wept anew because she hadn't known her sister at all. She found Edith's last web search. *Act of God.*

Had Edith found God? Their mother was a secular Jew. Their father's only religion was jazz, or so their mother told them. He died when they were three of a cerebral aneurism while soloing on his trumpet. Edith had always been adamant about her lack of faith, while Kat secretly hoped for miracles.

Over the next couple of days, Kat used the money from Edith's purse to buy one bottle of vodka after another. She didn't care what brand.

The BlackBerry rang sometime on the third day while Kat was reading Edith's datebook, weepy because Edith had so many friends. When the sacred BlackBerry rang, Kat almost believed that Edith was calling her from the other world.

"Katherine, it's Stanley Flom. I'm so sorry for your loss. Everyone here was so fond of Edith. You have our deepest condolences."

"Thank you," Kat said.

"I know this is a difficult time for you, but the medical examiner's office phoned me this morning. A decision has to be made. Edith wanted her body donated to science, but now that the preliminary autopsy is in, the ME doesn't think she'll be eligible."

"What did she die of? Was it her heart?"

"I didn't ask. You'll need to choose a funeral home."

Stanley might as well have told Kat that she needed to find an empty lot in Brooklyn and dig a grave. "Could you do that for me as her executor?"

"Certainly. Should we find a Jewish home? Was she religious?"

"I don't know."

"She left a letter for you in the event of her death. I imagine you don't want me to mail it. It's waiting for you anytime."

"Can I come now?"

"Of course."

As badly as Kat ached to read that letter, she didn't want to arrive for that solemn occasion in the rank crumpled clothes she'd been living in for three days. She stripped and showered, then put on Edith's pantsuit, the one Kat had worn to Sutton House in another life. It was still pouring out. She took a cab. To arrive by subway seemed disrespectful. In the elevator, riding up to Price, Bloodworth, Flom, Mead & Van Doren, a young woman, an attorney by the way she dressed, smiled at Kat and asked how she was enjoying her retirement. She must not have heard about Edith's death. "Hey, I like the blond do," she said.

The stately law office was hardly the anthill that Kat had imagined whenever she'd pictured Edith at work. She had never once visited her sister's beloved library, but then again, she had never been invited.

Stanley Flom's secretary Janice became teary when she saw Kat. "Edie was such a kind, generous soul. She will be dearly missed." She gave Kat a warm hug, and then opened Stanley's door.

Stanley was a tall, pudding-jowled man in his late seventies. He rose and stepped around his spotless desk to shake her hand. She noticed the envelope at once on his black leather desk pad. Stanley again offered his condolences, but Kat wasn't listening. She had gone to the place where the grieving go, an open field or the ocean's edge—hers was a rocky cliff—anyplace where there might be a promise of something out there, where one might confuse absence with presence.

He handed Kat the envelope.

"Do I read it now?"

"It's up to you. Would you like your privacy?"

"Yes, thank you."

She didn't immediately tear it open. She borrowed a silver letter opener from his desk so that she would do as little damage to the envelope as possible. Edith wouldn't be sending her another.

> My Dear Sister Kat,
>
> If you're reading this, I'm gone. I know you're grieving, but you'll be fine. You are a survivor. I have an important favor to ask. Please go in person to tell Alice Flom of my death. Go as soon as you can. I want you to tell her, not Stanley or anyone else. Please, Kat, I'm counting on you.
>
> With All My Love,
> Edie

Who was Alice Flom? Kat didn't remember Edith mentioning her. Alice had the same last name as Stanley. Was she his wife? The letter had no date, just the address of a nursing home in Westchester.

Stanley returned with Janice, who carried a pot of tea and two cups. He sat beside Kat, on the client side of the desk, in the second armchair. Why did Edith trust him as her executor yet not trust him to tell his wife of her death? Was he Edith's secret lover all these years? Was Alice her friend or rival?

"You haven't asked about the will," Stanley said.

Kat already knew what the will said. Edith had told her numerous times. She'd set up a trust for Kat, with an undisclosed sum, to begin payments on her sixty-fifth birthday. Even in death, Edith wanted to make sure Kat ate in old age.

As long as Edith's story was still evolving, she was alive for Kat. Outside the offices of Price, Bloodworth, Kat hailed a taxi. She gave the cabbie the nursing home address in Westchester, twenty miles north, an hour-and-a-half slog on the flooded expressway.

The cab pulled up to a bleak brick building on sumptuous grounds, as if a prison had been built in heaven. The Filipina nurse at the front desk said visiting hours were over, but when Kat told her about Edith's last request, she pointed Kat down the hall. "Third door on your right."

Alice didn't see Kat at first. She sat on a reclining chair, wearing a nightgown. She must have been ravishing when she was younger, but now, her facial skin looked as if it had been pinched and pinned up on her prominent cheekbones, like a pleated skirt. Her eyes, wet black river stones, appeared to be rapt in bliss, or captivated by nothing. But when she noticed Kat standing in her door, the vacant stare filled with suspicious bewilderment.

"Who are you?"

"Kat. I'm Edith's sister."

"Who's Edith?"

"You don't know?"

"Maybe I know, and maybe I don't, but I'll only tell if you promise to take me home with you."

"Where do you think my home is?"

"You live with your mother."

So she did know who Edith was after all. Alice's black

eyes—still wary, still befuddled—flooded with tears. Why would she cry for her rival? Maybe they were lovers? Was Edith gay? Wouldn't Kat have known, at least suspected? Why wouldn't Edith have told her? Kat walked toward Alice, who cringed like Kat meant to beat her. She sat down on the bed's edge and slowly offered Alice her hand. Alice took it in both of hers and examined Kat's palm, front and back, as if it were a gift box and Alice was supposed to guess what was inside. Kat intended to carry out Edith's last request even if poor Alice didn't understand. Edith was counting on her.

"Edith isn't with us anymore."

"Who's Edith?"

The play was supposed to have begun twenty minutes ago, but the inexhaustible rain, a constant for five days, wouldn't quit, though it had subsided enough to give false hope that it might abate long enough to have at least one performance. The expectant audience, despite a canopy of umbrellas, was now wet and shivering.

Costumed and made-up and ready to hit the boards, Vida, Edmund, and the Earl of Kent watched the Weather Channel on the Fool's iPad. Regan and Lear, married in real life, played gin for a dime a point, while the stage manager went outside for the third time. If the rains were abating, the surface of Turtle Pond, the small lake next to the stage, would calm down first. Canceling would be an easier call if the play were *Hamlet* or *Henry V.* The stage boards would be too slick for swordfights. But the only real stage violence in Lear, aside from the storm and a couple of stabbings, is the plucking out of Gloucester's eyes, and that could be accomplished without slipping on the wet boards. Cordelia, a television actress Vida found insufferably earnest and mediocre, strode into the dressing area and announced that the audience was waiting. "We can wear big fun hats to protect the mikes," she said.

"What kind of a big fun hat should the King wear to his own tragedy?" asked Regan, reshuffling her hand.

"Gin," said Lear dryly to his wife. "You now owe me one thousand sixty-six dollars and eighty cents."

"First Julia broke her teeth, and now this," said Edmund.

"I'm canceling the performance," said the stage manager.

Booing, louder than the rain, filled the dressing area, and all the actors turned toward the sound as if it had been directed at them personally. The stage manager must have just announced that the performance was canceled.

"Let's just get takeout," Regan said to Lear as he changed out of his kingly robes into his stretch-waist jeans.

"I'm wired, does anyone want to get a drink?" asked Cordelia.

"I'm going home, lighting up a fat joint, and watching TV," said Kent.

Vida caught a cab back to the hotel. When she initially made the reservation she hadn't known the hotel had a loud club off the lobby. There was always a throng of tattooed young waiting to get in. The club's entrance resembled a limestone cave's mouth. Inside, aquamarine light shimmered, like reflected water in an underground grotto. The elevator kept to the same blue theme and her corridor, also blue, was lit with concentrated halogen spots that made Vida feel as if she were stepping from one lily pad of light to another. When she finally reached her room, took off her shoes, and stretched out on the bed, she felt the club's music thrumming through the floor. The hotel was costing her a fortune, and today she learned that she wasn't going home anytime soon. The day after tomorrow, her house would be hermetically tented and disfigured with acid until every last spore of what her insurance agent now referred to as *The Supermold* was dead. The EPA had ordered an immediate burn because the infestation had spread to her adjacent neighbors. After forty-eight inches of rain in five days, her basement must have become a primeval swamp.

She reached for her cell phone and texted Sam, a former lover whose key she still had. He was doing *Othello* in London. They had met through Virginia and had once played husband and wife in Albee's *The Goat,* but when the run ended, their robust sex, without the goat, fizzled into friendship.

He answered her immediately.

GUESS WHO'S SLEEPING WITH DESDEMONA?????????
ME CASA SU CASA. SORRY ABOUT THE MESS.

She didn't know if he was referring to her situation or the cleanliness of his apartment. He lived in one of those posh new Williamsburg developments on the East River, only a few blocks from her home. She had looked at an apartment on the twelfth floor of the second tower before deciding on her old row house. She hadn't wanted to live so aseptically, in concrete and glass.

On the second floor of the first tower, she got off the elevator and unlocked Sam's door. He wasn't kidding about the mess. The entry floor was stained red. An open bag of pretzels, half-empty jars, and pineapple rind cluttered the small kitchen counter. A woman's black sleeveless dress, silk camisole, and jeans were hanging over the tub. Was he seeing someone and hadn't told her? Whoever she was had good taste, though Vida didn't care for the uniform red cast to all the fabrics. Only as she was changing the bed sheets did it strike her—didn't she own the exact same dress, camisole, and jeans? She left the bed unmade to check the labels. Her size. She slipped her hand into the jeans' left front pocket and her index finger found the familiar hole. Had she left some clothes at his house? She hadn't spent the night here in six months. Sam had been over for dinner a couple of weeks ago, had he stolen her clothes? Why would he steal her clothes? Why would he dye them red? Maybe she was making too much of a wild coincidence, albeit an unsettling one. He'd always said he admired her style. Why not expect him to be attracted to a new lover who had similar tastes? The clothes weren't exactly haute couture originals. She was a size eight, common enough. And doesn't everyone have a hole in her pocket?

Ashley hid in the broom closet when she heard someone open the front door. According to the hen's datebook, the actor wasn't supposed to return for a month. Whoever was inside walked with a light, female stride. When Ashley heard the bathroom door close, she quietly tiptoed out of the apartment, wearing only the actor's kimono. Her temples were pounding from startled flight, but she strolled down the hall as if she belonged there. She rode the elevator to the top floor. The penthouse key was on the ledge where the doorman had left it.

Closing the door behind her, the darkness was so abrupt and depthless that it looked as if someone had blacked out the three glass walls, or maybe the thirtieth floor was engulfed in the black clouds, or maybe it was raining oil. If a city was out there, she couldn't see it.

She didn't dare turn on any lights. Who knew who was watching? She groped her way across the vast nothingness, a blind beggar crossing the steppes, exposed to whatever hunts at night, unaware of the precipice ahead.

When she bumped into what she discovered was a bed, she climbed under the covers (there were no sheets), curled into a ball, and drew the spread over her head until the terrifying emptiness became only a sliver of darkness. Why had she come to this alien land? How had she ended up so alone?

Where was her mama? Everyone back in Omsk was right: she was an *insignificuntski,* she had no business thinking she could make it in America.

Self-disgust, like bile, rose from her gullet to her throat and she threw back the covers. By touch, she returned to the factory-sized living room, determined to learn how Americans experience stormy black nights. They sit comfortably on their deep, soft sofas, dry and safe, enjoying the rain's music. They don't cower like mice fearing unseen hawks overhead. Darkness isn't a hole you hide in; it's the cosmos.

The cab from the nursing home back to the Metropolitan Hotel cost Kat over a hundred dollars. She tried to pay with Edith's American Express card, but the card was denied. She gave the cabbie a fistful of cash from Edith's purse. On the way through the lobby, the night clerk, the kind Indian man who had found Kat a drink on that dreadful first night, asked if he could speak to her.

"Your sister's credit card has been frozen. Can we please have another one?"

Kat handed over Edith's Visa, Discover, and MasterCard, all denied. She paid cash for the night, leaving her only forty dollars and some coins. She had Edith's ATM card, but Edith hadn't shared the password. Why hadn't Edith trusted her with anything? Then she remembered her fuckup about the pills. No wonder Edith hadn't trusted her. But not to tell her who Alice was?

Kat hadn't let the maid into their room since Edith's death, but the maid had come today. Both beds were made. She suddenly missed the naked mattress. Tomorrow morning she'd see if one of the neighbors could take her in until her house was fumigated. She could always ask Frank, though maybe he was living with a lady these days? She looked over at Edith's bed, so foreign and false with its fresh white sheets, like a grassy park built over a landfill. She took out Edith's letter and reread it.

As little girls, they could guess each other's thoughts, and often played whole afternoons communicating in silence. But when they reached adolescence, Kat discovered boys, rock 'n' roll, and marijuana. She found it intolerable to share a bedroom, a bathroom, a wardrobe, and a face with her conformist sister.

Kat was necking with a boy behind the school gym one day when she glanced over and saw Edith watching from the bleachers, her features so judgmental that it felt, to Kat, as if Edith's face had accused hers of being a liar. Once Kat stopped being Edith's protector, the mean girls sensed her vulnerability. They bullied Edith on the way home from school one afternoon while Kat looked the other way. That evening, as their mother applied iodine to Edith's cut lip, Kat asked Edith's forgiveness in their secret twin language, but Edith pretended not to hear. It was days before she spoke to Kat, weeks before she trusted her—if she ever did again.

The sun finally came out after nine solid days of rain. In bright spokes of morning light, Kat returned to her old block, suitcase in hand. She'd left Edith's bag with the Indian clerk, pleading with him to keep it safe behind his desk until she knew where she was going. If Frank couldn't take her in, she'd ask Gladys. Gladys and Edith were close. She called Edie her adopted daughter. Didn't that make Kat a daughter, too?

She found Gladys sitting in her white van parked at the end of the block. Only after she rapped on the driver's window did she realize that Gladys had been asleep. Blinking bewilderedly, the old lady stared at the steering wheel, at her disheveled visage in the rearview mirror, at Kat's face in the window.

Kat gestured for her to roll down the glass, and Gladys cracked it an inch. "I can't open it any more or the cats will jump out. Blackie got loose this morning."

"What are you doing sleeping in your van?"

"We got evacuated yesterday. I found mushrooms growing in the cat litter. My niece invited me to spend the night but she's allergic to my cats. Where are we going to live?"

"Go to your niece's, get some proper rest. Leave the cats in the van. I'll feed them, or Frank will. It's only for a few days."

"It's forever. The HAZMAT chief called it a supermold. The city is burning down my house tomorrow. Where's Edith?"

"You don't know? She's gone. Edith is dead."

"Oh my god, oh my god." Gladys lifted the gold cross around her neck and kissed it. "Your sister is in heaven."

It was the first time that Kat hadn't been reduced to sobs when someone consoled her about Edith, and suddenly the need to tell every excruciating detail about that night came on her like a thirst. "She was fine when I left in the morning. We both had soft-boiled eggs from room service. We were staying at the Metropolitan. Edith died the day before the big storm . . . no, no, it was the first day of the storm. I remember thinking, when I woke up that morning, that the approaching thunderheads looked biblical. Her death must have been very sudden, she was in her bra and underwear. She looked so peaceful, I thought she was sleeping."

"Why does He always take the good ones first?" Gladys dropped the gold cross as if it had bit her and looked at

Kat with scarlet-rimmed, flooded eyes. "I thought Pippa was sleeping, too, but I don't believe for a minute her death was peaceful."

"Who's Pippa?"

"My Siamese. I found her three nights ago curled on her pillow. Pippa never shared her pillow with the other cats, but that morning, Billy lay beside her. Mushroom poisoning is a torturous way to die, don't kid yourself. And now, Missy looks sick."

"You think the cats ate the mushrooms?"

"Not Pippa. She was such a finicky queen. She would never have eaten a mushroom. She and Edith must have breathed in the same deadly spores."

Kat remembered Edith's glowing bed with the iridescent slime seeping out from under the bed skirt. How could she not have breathed in the spores? Her mattress was practically alive. They should have been evacuated weeks ago. They should have just up and left when Edith smelled that foul odor. "Do you know how many times Edith tried to warn Vida that this could happen?" She started to tell Gladys about the glowing mattress but stopped herself. Gladys had just lost her favorite cat. She didn't need to hear about a glowing mattress.

In the van's rear, fifteen agitated felines paced the tight space, avoiding a sickly creature with crusted yellow eyes. "The vet said Pippa died from old age, but now my two-year-old Missy has the same symptoms. Who's going to take in an old lady with seventeen cats? Sixteen," she corrected herself. "Will you look around for Blackie today? He might have tried to go home."

"I'll put out the word," said Kat.

She ran into Frank at the corner coffee shop. He didn't see her at first. He sat in a booth, relishing a jelly doughnut with his eyes closed. "You feeling okay?" he asked, when she sat down across from him. "You look like you haven't been sleeping too good."

"Edie is dead."

Frank must have endured stunning punches during his prizefighting years, because the two sides of his face no longer aligned. But that morning, when she told him the news, the shock momentarily set every feature straight, and Kat remembered what a handsome young man he had been.

He already had a big bite of doughnut in his mouth. He swallowed it as if it were a wad of hot chili. His eyes watered, and he used his napkin, dusty from sugar, to blow his nose. "Oh, Kat, I'm so sorry." He moved to her side of the booth and held her.

"Frank, I miss her so much."

"Course you do. You guys were twins. Edie was a grand lady. You know, she's the one who made Vida hire me. She was real worried about that smell in the basement. Vida should of listened to her."

"Gladys thinks the mushrooms killed her."

"I guess she told you about Pippa."

"Frank, can I stay at your place for a few days? I had to check out of the hotel."

"I guess you didn't hear. A whole bunch of us got evacuated yesterday. I'm sleeping on my cousin's sofa. I'll ask him, but his wife don't like me in the house as it is. She's worried I'm contaminated. She made me shower with DDT soap and she burned all my clothes."

"Your house, too? I'm sorry, Frank. Maybe Mrs. Syzmanski can take me in?"

"She can't. Mr. Syzmanski found a mushroom coming out of their kitchen drain this morning. Their building is being evacuated now."

Frank bought her a coffee and a doughnut to go, and carried her suitcase for her. The HAZMAT truck was double-parked in front of the Syzmanskis' six-story, walk-up tenement. The elderly couple and their tenants, in various increments of shock, staggered out, as if on anesthetized feet—a young bleach-blond Asian man in a germ mask carrying a passel of electronics, a middle-aged couple struggling with a stroller and a newborn, a heavily tattooed young woman carrying a screaming caged cockatoo. When she saw Kat, her expression hardened from distress to agitation to menace.

"You! You and your sister were the first to get the mushrooms! Their nest must be somewhere in your basement!"

"My sister is dead!"

Kat could have heard a pin drop if not for the police radios and the screaming cockatoo.

In the open windows of the uninfected buildings, worried neighbors watched and listened. Marty, the barrel-chested plumber who lived with his ninety-year-old mother in the house next to Gladys's, stood sentry duty on his stoop, as if the mushrooms couldn't enter without a password. He suddenly began hurling obscenities at the HAZMAT chief. "For fuck's sake, cut off the shithole water main and the piss-ass gas lines, and then burn down the goddamn infested houses before we all die."

"Listen to him," said his mother, standing beside her scarlet-faced son, "he's a licensed plumber."

The policewoman who had evacuated Edith and Kat only seven days before now herded the new refugees away from the condemned building.

"No one is really going to burn down our house, are they?" asked the middle-aged father, empty stroller in tow.

"Our baby might be poisoned?" asked the mother, clutching the newborn.

"We have rights," said the tattooed girl, carrying the flapping, shrieking white whirligig of caged feathers.

Kat approached the HAZMAT chief. All fell silent. After all, she was the elder of this tribe. She was their future.

"Did the mushrooms kill my sister?" she asked.

The chief took off his mask. "I'm sorry for your loss, but I don't know what happened to your sister." He turned back to his men, a dozen yellow-clad figures in hoods and masks. They were tramping across the roofs, lowering a gigantic yellow tent over the infested buildings.

"What are they doing?" asked the middle-aged father.

"It's a gas chamber," said Mrs. Syzmanski.

"What about all our stuff?"

"You want that stuff?" his wife asked.

"Yes, it's everything we own."

"It's infected. Her sister is dead. Our baby might be poisoned."

"Our mother's archives are inside," Kat told Frank.

"So are my old boxing gloves."

"You'd think Vida would be here."

"She's probably rehearsing," he said. "She's starring in some free Shakespeare play at Central Park tonight."

Gladys was coming down the street, passing out lost-cat flyers to anyone who would take one. "Have you seen my Blackie? Have you seen my Blackie?"

Kat tried to make a withdrawal from Edith's bank that afternoon. When the teller asked for picture identification, Kat presented Edith's driver's license. She didn't lie. She just didn't say she wasn't Edith.

The teller asked Kat to enter her PIN and then discreetly looked away.

"I'm so embarrassed, but I've forgotten it," Kat said.

The teller's nails clattered across her keyboard. "Your mother's maiden name?"

Kat told her.

"Your first pet."

Edith had had a hamster named Checkers.

The teller stopped typing, squinted at her screen, and then looked querulously at Kat. "It says here that your accounts are frozen in probate. Someone thinks you're dead."

The King is coming!

The orchestra's coronet played a brassy herald.

Vida and her sisters, Regan and Cordelia, marched up the stage ramp in step behind their father, King Lear. The first few seconds onstage, Vida didn't believe she was a queen any more than the lady in the front row, the one eating M&Ms, believed that *she* was one. A wracking cough in the audience shattered Vida's concentration, and she had to remind herself that wracking coughs were as common as fleas in pre-Roman Britain.

Some actors prepared for a role by learning everything there was to know about the character, the motivations, and the play's history, and some actors only wanted to know their own lines. Vida was the latter sort, as was her father the King, imperial despite a stamp of boorishness in his stride, an actor whose subtlety and pride gave Lear divine airs, lest anyone forget how powerful he was. Years ago, when Vida was an understudy for Perdita in *The Winter's Tale,* her first job in London, that same actor had played Leontes, the irrationally jealous King of Sicilia. Vida had heard that the great British actors, in order to prepare for a performance, went to the zoo to find a primate on which to base their role. Standing in front of the baboon house, she'd found the perfect Perdita, a young female whose haughty airs in no way hinted at her lowly status. She heard Leontes's distinct voice behind her. "When I play the King," he had said, pointing toward a lone male sitting on a rock and cleaning his genitals, "I'm that red-bummed one over there."

Tonight, he was most certainly King of the Baboons. Shakespeare didn't create individuals, Samuel Johnson said, he created species. Beneath Lear's boots, papering the entire outdoor stage, was the map of his kingdom. The designer had intended that the kingdom slowly shred and tear beneath the actors' feet in rhythm with the King's undoing, but after last week's record rainfall, the sodden paper was now as friable as old skin: the King's world would fall apart far faster than intended. Already pieces of the kingdom were sticking to the actors' shoes. The only prop onstage was an ornate chair.

As Lear took his throne, all of the members of the royal coterie dropped to their knees in unison, and prostrated, bums to the audience, foreheads to the ground, except Cordelia. The young television actress had no improvisational instincts, and in fear of tearing the map and further changing the course of the play, she remained standing a whole beat longer than her sisters. Vida and Regan exchanged incendiary, almost jubilant smiles. Now, in addition to pride, the King's favored youngest would be guilty of insolence. Lear spoke:

> Tell me, my daughters—
> Since now we will divest us both of rule,
> Interest of territory, cares of state—
> Which of you shall we say doth love us most,
> That we our largest bounty may extend
> Where nature doth with merit challenge.—Goneril,
> Our eldest born, speak first.

Vida spoke:

Sir, I love you more than word can wield the matter,
Dearer than eyesight, space, and liberty,
Beyond what can be valued, rich or rare,
No less than life, with grace, health, beauty, honor.
As much as child e'er loved, or father found,
A love that makes breath poor, and speech unable . . .

Vida entered the all-important pause—the ten heart-beats during which ruthlessness, wile, avarice, and betrayal must flit across her features—but all Vida could think about was that her beautiful old row house was going to be disfigured with acid tomorrow. She barely remembered her line.

Beyond all manner of so much I love you.

Just before coming onstage, she'd unwisely checked her voicemail in the dressing room. Virginia had promised to call if she made any headway with the insurance company, which was still refusing to pay. The only messages were from Edith, six new ones after having not heard from her in more than a week. She knew she should have listened to them and called Edith back, but she was already in character, her voice raspy with queenly arrogance, not a good tone in which to tell someone that her home and everything she owned was about to be burned and there was nothing anyone could do about it. She should have listened to Edith's fears all along.

The King was now stomping on his paper kingdom, railing against Cordelia for not oiling his vanity. The moment had come for Vida to take center stage again. Her father was about to give her half a monarchy, but his brutish footwork had completely destroyed it.

The Delacorte Theater, the open-air stage in Central Park's bowl of foliage, was still dripping from yesterday's deluge. Kat could see floodlights at the path's end, beacons in the damp and dark forest. She arrived as intermission was ending, just as the audience began funneling through the gates, back to their seats. All afternoon, she'd tried to reach Vida to see if anything could be done to save the letters in the basement before the burn tomorrow. She'd left at least half a dozen messages, but Vida never called back. She finally understood Edith's frustration. She'd been using Edith's BlackBerry. Maybe Vida thought the calls were from her? Did she even know that Edith was dead? It was one thing to have ignored her calls, but Edith's? How could Vida go onstage when Edith was dead?

She wasn't yet sure what she would say to Vida except *Edith is dead.*

The important point was that Vida be told. She shouldn't be allowed to go onstage and become absorbed in her role and transported to another realm without being aware of the suffering she had left behind in this one. Kat had always dreaded confrontations, but she knew that had it been she who had died and Edith who had lived, Edith would have damn well made sure Vida was held accountable, even if only emotionally.

Kat joined the lines of returning theatergoers. A plump woman in an unbecoming usher's blazer demanded to see her ticket. Left and right, others streamed past without producing a stub.

"Where are *their* tickets?" Kat asked.

"I remember them."

"All of them?"

"Yes."

Kat hadn't washed her hair in a week. Her eyes were puffy and bloodshot from nine days of grieving and drinking. One of her sandal straps had broken. She carried her worldly possessions in a shabby imitation-leather suitcase held together by duct tape. She didn't look like a theatergoer.

She waited on a park bench with a view of the entrance. About fifteen minutes before the play ended, the ushers abandoned their posts to watch the last act. Kat walked straight through the deserted gates. The stage was strewn with paper shreds, like the bottom of a hamster cage. Vida wasn't onstage, just a bereft old king and a young female corpse. Swaying on his knees and embracing the limp girl, he electrified his grief. The current ran through Kat's veins. Edith's death felt wholly shocking again.

As the clapping began, the actors, holding hands like paper-doll cutouts, swept onto the stage to take their bows. Hands covered in blood, Vida held the fingers of a beggar whose eye sockets were blackened and bloodied to look void. Had her character plucked out his eyes?

Kat called to her, but Vida didn't hear anything except the audience's escalating applause. The louder the adulation, the more beautiful and fulfilled she looked. The brighter her radiance, the sadder and angrier Kat became. It wasn't fair that Vida got to bask in glory while Edith lay in a morgue refrigerator. She started to make her way toward the stage, but the plump usher stopped her.

"If you don't leave this minute, I'll call security," she warned.

"I know one of the actresses, Vida Cebu."

"You're not on her list."

"You don't even know my name."

Having no choice, Kat returned to the park bench, which she now shared with a homeless man and his dog.

"Did you like the play?" he asked.

Vida was the last player to leave. The other actors had waited until the audience dispersed, then left as a group. Twenty minutes later, Vida walked out alone, cell phone to her ear. Her prideful radiance was long gone. She looked wan and agitated. Maybe she was finally listening to her messages? Kat rose from the bench, about ten feet ahead, and blocked her path.

"Edith?"

"Edith is dead."

"Oh my god. When? How did it happen?"

"She died the night after we fled your poisoned house. Her bed was glowing. If you'd returned her calls earlier, she might have gotten out in time. Why didn't you call her back?"

"Listen to me, Kat, I didn't know anything about the mushrooms until I found one in my closet. Did Edith's doctor tell you she died of mushroom poisoning?"

"There wasn't time to call a doctor."

"I'm very sorry about your sister. Is there anything I can do?"

"Can you help me save the letters in the basement?"

"I'm sorry, but no one can save anything. I wish I could help. Believe me, if I could stop the burn tomorrow I would."

"Why didn't you call her back?"

"Kat, no one's responsible. You have my deepest condolences for your loss, but no one could have predicted—not me, not the city, no one—that this was coming. It was an act of God."

"Don't blame this on God."

After Vida left, the theater lights went out. Kat remained in the dark forest. She hadn't made any plans past the confrontation. She should call Frank to see if his cousin had changed his mind about her spending the night, or if that didn't work out, she could always call Gladys and join her in the van, but the BlackBerry was dead from all the calls she'd made to Vida.

She walked to Grand Central, twenty blocks south, so she could charge the BlackBerry without having to waste money at a coffee shop. She had only thirty-four dollars left, plus the twenty Frank had given her.

Grand Central's terminal was surprisingly crowded for a midweek late night. The four-faced clock above the information booth read a quarter to midnight. She looked around for a free electric socket, but the commuters had all commandeered the plugs. Or were they commuters? None appeared to be unplugging anytime soon. Occupying the nearest socket, an older unshaven gentleman in a crumpled suit recharged his cell phone *and* his electric shaver. On the next bench, a middle-aged lady had set up a half-dozen gadgets to suckle power from a surge protector. Who commutes with a surge in her purse? Had she found mushrooms in her closet? Fortressed behind three big suitcases, a little man slept on a bench with his head atop his recharging laptop. He'd removed his shoes. Had he woken up in a glowing bed? They weren't here to catch a train any more than she was.

She found an open outlet near Track 101. After plugging in, she must have dozed off, because the next time she looked over at the four-faced clock, it was six a.m. She washed her face and hair in the ladies' room and dried herself under the hand blower. At the next sink, the woman with the surge protector in her purse brushed her teeth.

She rode the express train back to Brooklyn. She still might be in time to save the letters if she could just persuade the HAZMAT chief that the archive wasn't contaminated. Edith had kept the letters in hermetically sealed, double-strength plastic containers. Maybe the containers could be burned and the archive saved? She'd explain to the chief how invaluable the letters were, that they were going to the Smithsonian next month to become part of the National Archives.

The pale morning sun had just cleared the roofs by the time she emerged from the subway. Gladys's van was still parked at the corner, her sleeping profile silhouetted in the driver's window, a cat on her shoulder. A bright yellow three-story-high and half-a-block-wide tent covered the row houses. A truck with a baby-whale-sized cylinder was parked in front. A thick hose ran from a valve on the tank to a fitting in the tent. Kat could see that something was happening within. The plastic kept inflating and deflating, as if the row houses were fighting for breath.

Frank was the only soul around. Hands dug in pockets, he faced the yellow enormity, his expression bearing the anguished surprise of a man who has just turned around to find a three-story-high wave about to crash over him.

"Am I too late? Is it over?" Kat asked. "Our mother's archives are still inside. Edie would be devastated."

"You couldn't have done nothing anyway. The acid they're using can eat an entire SUV in less than six hours. By tonight, our homes will be ash, like nobody ever lived there. I know those buildings like I'd built them myself, and now all that knowing's going to be useless. Where are we supposed to go?"

"I wish I knew."

"You wonder why those sad sacks on the Jersey Shore are rebuilding in exactly the same spot after the ocean tore away their last homes. Where else they going to go?"

Kat tried to locate the spot where she imagined her front door was, the one that would always open for her no matter how far she strayed. Heat waves rippled off the plastic. The seams appeared to be melting. The tent was a gas chamber, just as Mrs. Syzmanski had predicted.

All the letters—*Abused, Bewildered, Compromised, Damned, Ebullient, Fuming, Guilty, Humbled, Infatuated, Jilted, Kinky, Loveless, Manipulated, Nervous, Obstinate, Petrified, Queasy, Ridiculed, Shadowed, Teased, Unloved, Vilified, Wistful, Xenophobic, Yearning, Zealous*—asphyxiated.

Not all the letters. There were three hundred survivors. In her bereavement, she had almost forgotten about the manuscript. Thank god she hadn't listened to the editor and winnowed the pages to under a hundred. The manuscript must be on his desk. Maybe he had been trying to reach her all week with good news? It would be such a tribute to Edith and her mother if the letters were published.

"Frank, I have to leave now to take care of something important."

He watched warily as she picked up her suitcase. "Are you coming back?"

She suddenly didn't know. What was left for her to come back to?

Kat waited in the reception area at Sutton House for her affable editor to come out of his office to greet her like last time. She wanted a contract or she wanted the manuscript back. She perched on the leather sofa adjacent to a wall-length, glass-fronted bookcase and crossed her ankles to conceal the broken sandal strap. She could see her messy reflection in the spotless glass. The shelves were bricked solid with colorful spines so straight and orderly compared to the chaos and devastation only a subway ride away. About ten minutes later, his assistant, the young lady who had brought Kat a coffee with two sugars during her last visit, appeared with the survivors, still safe in their three-ring binder.

"He wants you to have these back. There's a letter inside."

"There are three hundred letters. What does his say?"

"I don't know," she lied.

Kat removed the envelope. She didn't finish reading the rejection. She crumpled it into a ball and dropped it at her feet.

She needed a drink.

Crossing Fifth Avenue, she returned to the garnet-red bar where she'd met Lenny and ordered vodka, a double. Shaken by the rejection and the feeling that she'd let Edith and her mother down, she opened the binder and leafed reverently through the pages, stopping to reread the last letter, "Bereft in Plattsburg." The young widow who wrote so lightly you could barely make out her question. *Will I find love again?* She had chosen that letter to close the volume so that the reader was left weeping. The editor was blind. These letters were extraordinary. She'd make sure they got to their new home at the Smithsonian, but where would she go? Back to California? She imagined herself returning to the trailer in the primeval redwood forest whose massive trunks held up heaven. She wanted so badly to return to her old carefree, careless self.

Three doubles later, she staggered to Grand Central to find an empty bench for the night. The evening rush hour was just ending. She sat on both the manuscript and the BlackBerry so that no one would steal them, and then tucked her suitcase between her knees.

She'd just closed her eyes when someone clapped stridently next to her ear. "You can't sleep here," said a policeman.

"I must have dozed off. I'm recharging my BlackBerry."

"Where'd you get that?"

"It's my dead sister's."

"You sure about that?"

He reached for the phone, but Kat wouldn't let go.

"Lady, how much did you drink today?"

His partner, two benches down, was rousting a rag bundle. "Up and at 'em." The officer poked the pile with his nightstick. Two swollen, cracked, filthy feet emerged and began to stir.

"You, too," Kat's policeman said.

She was herded into a knot of homeless and shooed out of the terminal. One of the men, a rather charming old salt, invited her to spend the night at his "country estate," a mattress he kept hidden behind a bush in Central Park. She declined.

She just wanted to go home, even with no home to go to.

In an all-night Laundromat, Ashley heard a ruckus behind her. She'd been stuffing a pillowcase with some other girl's freshly dried clothes. The girl had stepped outside for a smoke. In the washing machine area, the night manager was shooing away a homeless woman who had tried to recharge her cell phone in one of the laundry's sockets.

American beggars have cell phones? Who do beggars call? Who calls them?

"You can't sleep here stealing my electricity!" the manager shouted.

"I have every right to be here," the beggar said. "My clothes are still in the dryer."

"Show me which one?"

"Okay, my clothes aren't in the dryer right now. They're in my bag, but I laundered them here earlier. I paid good money and I have every right to sit here." She started to open her ratty suitcase to prove to the manager that her clothes were clean.

"Lady, I don't want to see your dirty underwear."

While all eyes were on the commotion, Ashley hoisted the overstuffed pillowcase, hiding behind its bulk, so that when she snuck past the girl smoking in the doorway, all the girl would see was a fat pillow atop two comely legs.

Halfway down the street, she heard the beggar call, "Ashley?"

She about-faced. She barely recognized Kat under the street lamp, hobbling on a broken sandal. The old twin had fared worse than she had. Her suitcase was belted with duct tape, her clothes looked slept in, her blond hair was matted and jutting, like a picture Ashley once saw of sun flares. There was nothing to be gained in befriending her. She surreptitiously glanced at Kat's white-knuckled hand, clutching the cell phone. She could easily snatch it and run, but she didn't. Kat remained the only person in America who had talked to her "on par."

"So how best seller doing? You still need Russian translator?" Ashley asked.

"When can you start?"

"I check schedule. How life at Metropolitan Hotel?"

"It's a long story. Are you still house-sitting for the actor?"

"Lousy view. I move up to penthouse. Plenty of electricity. Much juice as phone can drink."

"Does the penthouse also have a bath? Oh, Ashley, I would do anything to take a long hot soak and get out of these filthy clothes."

"Electricity costs."

"How much?"

"Five dollars."

"I can find my own plug, thank you."

"Price include hot bath and clean bed."

Kat gave her four ones and a fistful of coins.

"Here are rules. We tell doorman you American grandmother come for visit."

"No one will believe I'm a grandmother. Let's tell him I'm your aunt."

.   .   .

"I move to penthouse week ago," she told Kat as she retrieved the key from the door ledge. She didn't immediately turn on the lights as they stepped inside. She wanted Kat to see the unimpeded bejeweled skyline.

"Two-million-dollar view," she quoted one of the real estate brokers she'd overheard while hiding in the closet.

Kat smiled, her enormous false teeth as bright as a miner's lamp. "You've done very well for yourself, Ashley."

"This model apartment. I house-sit for her. She think maybe I be model, too."

"Oh, Ashley, you don't have to pretend with me. I know you're squatting. Point me toward the tub. You don't happen to have any bubble bath, do you?"

While Kat soaked, Ashley plucked her dirty, rank pantsuit off the bathroom tiles, as if it were an infected hankie, and carried it to the trash chute. She didn't want those rags on her clean floor. Just as she tossed it into the blackness, she saw, or thought she saw, a tiny comet of luminous spores. It twinkled only for a split second.

After washing her hands twice in the kitchen sink, she sat by the wall of glass to wait for Kat to finish. Until tonight, she hadn't talked to another soul in close to a week. She watched the river far below, a black crevasse between two incandescent glass cliffs. The view had only saddened her until now. She wished she had a picture of herself in front of the skyline to send back to Omsk. What good was beauty with no one to share it? Alone, beauty was almost cruel.

A blackout slammed over the steamy city, like a lid on a boiling pot.

The audience let loose a collective gasp as they waited for the lights to come back on.

The wind machine's blades made one last rotation. Becalmed on the black stage, the two old pros, Lear and Gloucester, finished their scene with such vociferous authority that the audience saw Gloucester's blindness.

Acts four and five continued by torch and candlelight, as a castle in pre-Roman Britain should be lit.

Afterward, in the dark dressing rooms, a communal bunker under the bleachers, the blind cast bantered and laughed, the infectious headiness of having surpassed the previous performances. Vida momentarily forgot that her home and everything she owned had been reduced to ash that morning. Unbuttoning her high-necked gown, she felt glorious. Beams from smartphones began to light up here and there. By touch alone, she changed into her street clothes.

"Are those sequined pants?" asked Regan.

She glanced down at the flecks of luminosity playing over her legs. Had she put on someone else's khakis? She reached into her pocket and fingered the familiar shape of her nail clipper, her talisman: she always trimmed her nails before a performance. The khakis were her favorite old pair, the only article from her contaminated wardrobe that she hadn't thrown away—she'd washed the pants twice with bleach. The longer she stared at the sequins, the more plentiful the spangles became, as if breeding before her eyes. The sequins were alive! She half screamed, half retched, then practically tore off her pants and T-shirt. One of the knights shined his smartphone on the commotion. The beam caught something alive and glowing in the back of Vida's dressing room.

The knight screamed.

Lear ordered all the knights to shine their smartphones on the glow, then knelt to take a closer look. "I believe Vida's growing mushrooms in her dressing room."

"How could mushrooms *not* be growing in this damp, hot dungeon?" asked Regan.

"Call the fire department," Vida told the stage manager.

"For a mushroom?"

"Ask for the HAZMAT squad."

While the stage manager dialed 911, Vida explained to the cast about the new supermold, and how she had lost her home.

"I believe I'll wait for the HAZMAT squad outside," said Lear, backing away from the toxic glow.

Rank was suddenly forgotten; queen and scullery maid, duke and pawn stampeded as a single blind herd into the night. The city was gone, the power outage vast. The normally starless New York sky now looked like a gala show at a planetarium.

Stripped to her bra and underwear, Vida sat away from the others, shivering on the bleachers, though the temperature hovered near ninety. She'd been wearing those contaminated pants all day, next to her skin. She'd put her hands in those infested pockets and then rubbed her eyes.

Headlights swept through the blackness, vectoring on the open-air theater. Trucks rumbled up to the gates, next to the ticket windows. Strobes suddenly blinded the players and crew. A dozen or so men, all hooded and hermetically sealed, began ducking under the bleachers, entering the dressing rooms.

The stage manager approached the hood giving orders, and then pointed at Vida. The hood turned to look. Vida recognized the HAZMAT chief's face in the clear plastic window. There was no sign of the *grin*.

"We're going to need you to step into the fumigation tent," said one of his suited squad, a woman.

Outside the theater, between the four-thousand-watt searchlights and the cordoned-off curious crowd, Vida felt as if she were at a premiere, in her bra and panties. Some of the onlookers recognized her, and not as Queen Goneril. People began aiming their smartphones at her, taking pictures and shooting videos.

The fumigation tent, lined with showerheads, resembled a car wash.

Without removing her hood, the woman asked Vida to undress, then sealed Vida's bra and panties in a biohazard bag. Vida then stepped into the shower area; ten jets sprayed her from all directions. The woman asked her to hold up her arms and then scrubbed Vida raw with what felt like an industrial-sized push broom. Before Vida was allowed to towel off, the woman coated Vida with chemical-smelling talc from what looked like a fire extinguisher. Still naked, Vida was led to a water fountain that squirted her in the eye. Afterward, the woman had Vida look up and administered drops.

"You're fumigating my eyes?"

"It's perfectly safe."

Vida's fingernails and toenails, underneath and around the cuticles, were swabbed with a Q-tip that smelled of bleach.

"Should I see my doctor?" Vida asked, as the woman used another Q-tip to disinfect the whorls of Vida's ears.

"Do you have symptoms?"

"What should I be looking for?"

"Headaches, nosebleeds, fatigue, trouble breathing, coughing up blood, hair loss, rashes, swollen glands, memory loss, vomiting."

Vida involuntarily touched her neck glands. Were they swollen? She couldn't remember what size her neck glands normally were. Her arms smoldered and itched, but she saw no rash. Nausea fisted in her stomach. Was she about to vomit? If she didn't have a headache before, she had one now.

The woman issued Vida an orange jumpsuit, the kind worn by prisoners, and a pair of plastic clogs. When she emerged from the tent, all the other cast and crew sported orange jumpsuits too.

"The theater's being closed," announced the stage manager.

"How are we supposed to get home?" asked Regan. "All our money and credit cards are sealed in biohazard bags."

"Everyone will be issued Red Cross debit cards," explained the stage manager.

"What about our house keys?"

"Can't the doorman let you in?"

"I don't have a doorman," said Gloucester.

"You can't call a neighbor?"

"All our neighbors' numbers are in our confiscated phones."

"You'll have to call a locksmith," answered the exasperated manager.

"With what?"

Outside the park, traffic moved a block an hour. No cabs were available in any case. The subways were paralyzed. At the station entrances, bodies poured out of the stifling black underworld. Vida joined a sweaty herd pressing downtown. Here and there, a cold fluorescent street lamp blinked eerily above. Someone lit a cigarette.

"Put that out!" a flurry of voices shouted.

"You going to arrest me?" the smoker taunted. "It's a blackout. I'm going to smoke a goddamn cigarette in my own city if I damn well please. Fuck the mayor!"

Match flares, distant campfires in the dark night, sparked up here and there as smokers lit up.

By the time Vida reached Brooklyn, her new plastic clogs had given her what felt like trench foot. Was that one of the symptoms?

A red dot, the glass tower's emergency light, guided her toward the entrance. She blindly climbed the stairwell to the second floor, found the right door by counting knobs. Despite fatigue, she didn't go straight to bed. By touch, she opened every closet in Sam's apartment, anyplace she might have kept those infested pants, hunting for the phosphorescent spores. The unbroken blackness became the most beautiful color she could imagine.

A relentless bell woke her the next morning. The intercom was trilling. All the clocks in Sam's apartment blinked noon. The electricity was back on. Naked and half asleep, she answered the intercom.

"This is Jerzy from the front desk. Management is asking everyone to evacuate. The fire department is on its way."

Where's the fire? she was about to ask when the truth slapped her.

"Some kind of toxic mold has been found in the trash bins," said the doorman.

She put on last night's orange jumpsuit and plastic clogs, proof she'd already been decontaminated, hoping against hope she'd be spared the showers. Anything but. She was scrubbed, fumigated, and issued a new orange jumpsuit and another hundred-dollar Red Cross debit card. After she dressed, she was led into a second tent for a chest X-ray and then asked to wait on a folding chair.

A HAZMAT official dressed in a soupy shirt and loose tie opened a city map and had Vida show him the exact route she had taken on the previous night.

"Did you stop anywhere along the way? You came straight here?"

"Yes."

Holding his phone so that she could see the screen, he showed her a picture of a gray bundle (by color or dirt, she couldn't tell) and asked if the pantsuit was hers.

"No."

"This pantsuit has never been to the Delacorte Theater?"

"Not on me. Maybe it belonged to someone in the audience."

"You own 66 Berry Street in Brooklyn? Your tenants are Edith and Katherine Glasser?"

"One of the sisters is dead."

"Do you have a current address for Katherine Glasser?"

He hadn't bothered to ask her which sister had died: he already knew.

"Did you move your belongings directly from 66 Berry Street here? Where are those belongings now?"

"Upstairs."

"Nowhere else?"

"There's nothing left."

Finally released, Vida walked past police sawhorses, corralling scared, angry neighbors whose houses stood in the infested tower's shadow.

"What are you doing to protect our homes?" a man's baritone boomed over the grumbling.

"I warned you people last year about the infested Chinese drywall," someone else shouted.

"It's because of the old oil spill," a third joined in. "The mutant seeds grew in the petroleum."

"Yeah," the baritone boomed again. "The flooding from Sandy just brought them to life."

With her newly issued Red Cross card, Vida went to buy a prepaid cell phone with a thousand minutes. At the electronics store, she borrowed scissors from the cashier to cut the phone free from its packaging, but when she turned it on, nothing happened.

"You need to go home and charge the battery," explained the saleswoman.

The last time Vida had seen her home the tent was still up. Nothing bandaged it today. Her beautiful turn-of-the-century row house was now ash black and glassless, a coal miner's face without eyes. In the empty sockets, sunlight crisscrossed the interior, soot swirling skyward, like cigarette smoke in a nightclub's spotlight. She walked up the stoop, her plastic clogs leaving footprints in the ash. All that remained of the hundred-year-old front door with its original glass oval was a charred doorknob at her feet. She couldn't step inside. The foyer floor was gone. She looked up to where her roof once was. All that was left were joists, the ceiling bars of a cage.

Yet she felt oddly free, as if she'd escaped. Had the house been that much of a responsibility? Why didn't she feel worse? She took her emotional temperature. It was a little above normal, but that was always true the morning after a great performance, and last night's was definitely one of her best. The intensity of losing her home had heightened her creativity. Up until the moment the electricity went out, she had only been pretending to be a queen who had lost everything. But in that first panic after the darkness, she understood. Loss was far more complicated than the embittered defeat her performance was exhibiting. For the remainder of the play, her ruthless queen also had the insight of compassion.

The stage manager had promised to try to get the production moved to Prospect Park. If she still had her work, if she still had the possibility of matching—maybe even surpassing—last night's performance, she could get through anything, even this.

In a nearby coffee shop, she plugged in and dialed Virginia to see if the stage manager had called.

"I guess you already know," Virginia said when she heard Vida's voice.

"Know what?"

"You haven't seen it? The YouTube starring you? Some iPhone auteur filmed you in your bra and underwear being led into a decontamination tent by a guy dressed as if he's about to clean up Fukushima's Reactor 3. That's only the half of it. The footage is intercut with clips from your commercial. I got a call from Ziberax's attorney this morning. Pfizer is considering pulling the ad if the video goes viral. I'm sorry, Vida, I'll do what I can."

She sat down at a dirty table—milky dregs in a coffee cup and an untouched scone. She ate the scone. She hadn't eaten since yesterday.

At the next table, a slow game of solitaire played on an iPad. She asked the tablet's owner, an unshaven young man masticating a blueberry muffin, if she could borrow it, just for a moment. He stared at her orange prison jumpsuit and then suspiciously handed it over.

The YouTube clip opened with scenes from her commercial—the lovely beach house, her character's brittle responses to her playful husband, the doctor visit, the post-coitus close-up, intercut with handheld footage of her, practically naked. A rubber-suited, respirator-clad escort led her into a decontamination tent marked with biohazard, radioactive, and infectious disease symbols. Vida had never before seen herself on film when she hadn't been acting—even in home movies, she acted. The real Vida looked very much like her childhood self—wide-eyed, gap-mouthed.

A male voiceover began: "Ziberax side effects may include radioactive urine, transmittable pustules on or near the labia, swelling and peeling of the tongue, bloody saliva, blistered nipples, toxic breath, glowing discharge, and vaginal fungus."

There were now over a million hits.

Just like last time, Kat grabbed the irreplaceable letters and clutched them to her chest after the respirator-clad HAZMAT man gave her and Ashley five minutes to evacuate the penthouse. She would love to have saved Edith's pantsuit as well, but Ashley had thrown it down the garbage chute last night. She could hear drawers and cupboards banging in the other rooms as Ashley stuffed her pillowcase with everything she could cram inside—the model apartment's dinner plates, napkins, napkin rings, the tablecloth, the candleholder, a vase, and the faux laptop.

Yesterday evening, when Kat had finally emerged from the life-restoring hot bath, she'd found Ashley in the dark living room, transfixed by the window, unaware of her presence. The puzzling girl stood haloed in the city's afterglow, tiny and vulnerable against the pulsing skyline. Kat had sensed that Ashley had taken her in as much for the company as the money. She had to be a lonely but very brave girl, thought Kat. She'd come all by herself to America to be enchanted by those lights. Kat couldn't help but remember her own younger self, a girl hankering after glory. Then the city went abruptly black.

This morning, clutching the letters, she tried to get Ashley to evacuate, but the stubborn girl wouldn't leave until her pillowcase was as lumpy and heavy as a sack of potatoes.

Just when she thought she might have to drag her out, Ashley jammed one last towel into her distended sack and followed Kat down the thirty flights of service stairs with the other fleeing residents. The elevator had been shut off. On the ground floor, Kat turned to join the lines of stunned evacuees waiting to be decontaminated, while Ashley continued down to the basement exit. Kat followed her for a few steps, pleading with her to reconsider. "Ashley, if Edith had been properly decontaminated, she might be alive today."

"I be alive, but in Omsk."

"I'll tell them you're my niece."

"Who believe homeless woman. I keep stuff."

"No possession is worth dying over."

"You think Chernobyl cleanup guys let you keep old letters? No way. They burn Mama's book, then push you in chemical shower. Even false teeth brushed with bleach."

Kat handed Ashley the letters. "Don't let anything happen to them, please," she said, wondering if she'd ever see them again. "Where will we meet?"

"I find you."

Outside the lobby, a pop-up containment zone with two orange double-garage-sized decontamination tents blocked the street, one for men and one for women. The number of HAZMAT trucks and teams had quadrupled since Mr. Syzmanski's building was evacuated only three days ago. Kat got into the women's line.

She was stripped and scrubbed down by a tired nurse. The nurse must have washed at least the four dozen women before her.

"I think you missed a spot on my back," Kat said, reaching behind to direct her. "This is my second evacuation in two weeks. Last time, no one bothered to decontaminate me or my sister, and now she's dead."

"Where did you live before?"

"Sixty-Six Berry Street."

"Your name?"

"Katherine Glasser."

After she was sprayed, swabbed, and X-rayed, the nurse issued her an orange jumpsuit and told her to dress and wait there. Ten minutes passed before a man in a crumpled, sweat-soaked shirt and unknotted tie holding a crisp manila folder appeared, more than enough time to read a chest X-ray.

"Did you see anything on the X-ray?" Kat asked, assuming the film was in hand.

"Sorry, I'm a doctor of public health, not a radiologist," he said.

"Am I going to die? This is my second exposure to the mold. Did my sister die of mushroom poisoning, and is it just taking longer to kill me?"

"Your sister was Edith Glasser? You lived at 66 Berry Street?"

"I already told the nurse where we lived. When do I get my questions answered?"

"Your sister died of an ischemic stroke from a pulmonary embolism most likely caused by fungal pneumonia."

"But she didn't have any symptoms."

"Sometimes people don't."

Kat involuntarily clutched her chest in anguish over Edith's suffering, and in terror that her brain might flood any minute, too. The man assured Kat that if the radiologist had seen any sign of fungal pneumonia, let alone an embolism, she'd already be in an ambulance on her way to the hospital.

"Thank you," she said.

He angled his smartphone so that Kat could see the picture on his screen, a gray heap of mildew, a fistful of mush-rooms punching a hole out.

"Is the pantsuit yours?"

"Yes. No. It might be my sister's."

"Where are the rest of her belongings now?"

"The Metropolitan Hotel is holding her suitcase for me."

"I'm sorry to tell you this, but the Metropolitan and everything in it is scheduled to be burned tomorrow. Do you know how your sister's pantsuit wound up in this building's basement?"

"My niece threw it down the trash chute."

"Are your belongings still in your niece's apartment?"

"What belongings? I've lost everything."

Kat sat on a bench by the river. She no longer owned a watch, but she knew she'd been waiting more than two hours for Ashley to find her. The sun was now a pillar of flame between two distant skyscrapers. Just as she started to panic that Ashley had disappeared with the letters, she heard a thick Russian accent say, "Orange for sure not your color."

Clad in a new stolen dress, Ashley stood by the railing, the letters safe in her hands. "Surprised see me?"

"Just happy you found me. Oh, Ashley, you were so right. The letters would have been confiscated and destroyed." With gratitude, she opened her hands for Ashley to give her the binder, but Ashley threatened to drop the letters into the racing current.

"I swap for Red Cross gift card."

"You think I wasn't going to share the money with you?"

"Yeah, for sure."

"Yes, I would have," Kat said, and she meant it.

"You think two live on hundred dollars? How long?"

"We could help each other."

"BlackBerry, too."

"Why are you doing this? I thought we were friends."

Ashley jiggled the letters over the railing until Kat gave her the card. To prove to Ashley that she no longer had Edith's phone, she turned her jumpsuit pockets inside out.

"I have nothing left of Edith's but that book." She held out her empty hands again. She couldn't accept that Ashley didn't possess a penny's worth of compassion. "Please."

The heaviness of those letters as Ashley dropped them into her grasp, a weight the editor had found too much, was the most comforting burden Kat had ever held.

After Ashley left without so much as a good-bye, Kat watched the last spokes of daylight roll behind the skyline. She had only wanted to take the lost girl with her to the emergency shelter. One had been opened in a nearby school gymnasium for the growing number of evacuees. But now that she had the letters, she worried they'd be taken from her. No one was allowed to bring any personal items to the shelter—not clothes, not photographs, not even a toothbrush.

She knocked on Gladys's van window, hoping to leave the letters with her. The noise startled the poor woman and she abruptly sat up, once again trying to comprehend where in the world she was. Kat glanced over at the vinyl console. A lipstick tube and a can of aerosol deodorant shared the cup holder. The floor was thick with cats.

"Gladys, they've finally opened an emergency shelter. That's where I'm headed now. Come with me. We'll have showers and a hot meal and clean sheets. Maybe we'll finally find out what the city has planned for us. There must be hundreds of us mold refugees by now. The mayor must have a strategy. You can't stay here."

"I already asked. It's a no-pet shelter. I can't just leave my cats. They'll be scared at night without me."

"Why don't I keep you company until the cats fall asleep and maybe you'll change your mind," Kat said, climbing into the passenger seat.

"My babies are good company but it's nice to talk to a person for a change. Can I get you something to drink? I have Diet Coke," Gladys said, opening an ice chest behind her in the van's rear.

Kat thirstily drank the saccharine brown effervescence while Gladys fixed her a lunch meat sandwich, with a swipe of mustard. While Kat ate, Gladys picked up the binder and leafed through the pages.

"Are these the letters Edith always talked about? She told me they were off to the Smithsonian. Edith was so smart and accomplished, just like your mother. You could always count on her for good advice." She looked beseechingly at Kat as if Kat might miraculously transfigure into her sister. "Things are getting very tense back there. George can't bear the sight of Mona anymore. They don't stop fighting. I don't know what to do?"

It took Kat a second to realize that Gladys was asking about her cats.

"Maybe you could blindfold them?"

"I could try. I could use those cones cats wear after surgery. At least they wouldn't have to look at each other all the time."

Kat tilted her head back against the pillowed headrest and struggled to stay awake to listen to the rest of Gladys's feline soap opera. She must have momentarily dozed off, because when she next opened her eyes, infinitesimal diamonds of light, Las Vegas as seen through an airplane window on a cloudless night, scintillated on the console where Gladys had put the letters before falling asleep herself. The binder was sparkling, as if a schoolgirl had adorned it with glitter. She opened the cover. The paper was alive with spores. She almost flung open the door to hurl the book into the night, but all that would have accomplished would be to spread more spores and set loose the cats. Gladys would wake up alone. She knew what had to be done.

Taking Gladys's lighter and the manuscript, she quietly slipped outside and walked until she found an ash-blackened oil drum under the expressway.

After three or four tries with the lighter, the archival plastic sleeves began to melt while the acrid smoke crept and curled underneath the bubbling transparencies, blackening the half-century-old lunch counter placemat and the Plaza stationery, the brown bag and the length of toilet paper. Sparks popped and sizzled until the binder finally exploded into a bluish flame. The flame answered all the questions. *Will I find love again? Why did she lie to me? How could my husband sleep with my sister? Am I lovable?*

She could stand to think that life's experiences, good and bad, died with the body, but she couldn't bear to believe that dreams vanished too, those exquisite flights of reverie that never actually happened. All those experiences you can have for free. How could they burn and turn to ash? She would disappear one day, too, both her flesh and the woman she dreamed herself to be.

Without Edith, she had to accept the strangeness and solitude of existence.

.   .   .

Kat returned to the van to make sure that Gladys didn't wake up alone and disoriented. She gently stirred the befuddled woman awake. "It's time to go to the Red Cross shelter, Gladys."

"What about my cats?"

"They'll be thrilled to have the van all to themselves for a change. You need some human company."

"You think?"

"I know."

It's not every day that you're needed.

She and Gladys had to pass by their old block, bad enough with the blighted row houses, but now the trees were winter-bare, the sidewalk ankle deep in leaves though fall was still two weeks away. Looking up at the normally verdant elm that had shaded her stoop for a century, Gladys said, "I guess a tree can no longer grow in Brooklyn."

A guard let them into the school while a volunteer, wielding a flashlight, guided them through a basketball court lined with cots. Her beam landed on two empty ones. Gladys, who hadn't slept in a bed for days, immediately sank into snoring, but not Kat. She looked around the encampment. Blanketed bodies tossed and twisted in the reddish glow of exit lights. She recognized many of her neighbors sleeping in donated pajamas—the Syzmanskis, Marty the plumber from next door, but not Frank. What could they be dreaming about? Over the snores, she heard someone, Marty she thought, keening in his sleep. His mother had died shortly after Edith.

That night, for the first time since Edith died, she was waiting for Kat in sleep's foyer.

"I have so much to tell you," Kat said.

After not having so much as a kopeck in her pocket ever since she came to this country, the hundred-dollar card and the bulging pillowcase seemed like a fortune to Anushka Sokolov, but Ashley knew better. Without the names and addresses from hen's Rolodex—long gone—she had no idea where to go. Even in her panic, she was tempted to buy something pretty in one of the shop windows, or if she couldn't afford pretty, sugary. In cafés, rich young Americans dressed up in pretend rags and slurped frothy iced coffees. She noticed bowls of ice water set out for the dogs. She was thirsty. Was she supposed to get down on her hands and knees and lick from a bowl? She passed a window display of petrified noodles and fish, a shop that only sold lamps made from pop bottles and hangers, a juice bar that served liquid wheat, a store that sold hundred-year-old peasant furniture for thousands of dollars, an organic ice cream truck serving scoops the size of winter cabbages. A bicyclist, juggling a cell phone and a triple scoop, nearly pedaled into Ashley. His three chocolate balls splattered on the sidewalk. Good! Why does he get ice cream and not her?

She passed the long night riding subways, the gift card deep in her pocket, the pillowcase locked between her knees. By midnight, the commuters had thinned out. On her third round-trip to Brighton Beach, she had a car all to herself except for a middle-aged couple and a widow-peaked young wolverine in white slacks so tight and revealing, he looked like he wore sausage skins. Closing her eyes, she pretended she was in a first-class train compartment on her way to Hollywood or Las Vegas, rather than in a dirty boxcar burrowing under Brooklyn.

"Knock, knock, can I enter your daydream?" he asked. His English was thick and syrupy. He had a Muscovite accent.

"Het," answered Anushka.

"Where did an American girl like you learn Russian?"

Each syllable chimed in her ears with startling clarity. She hadn't heard a word of Russian, let alone a whole sentence, since arriving in this country noisy with growls, hoots, yowling, caws, hisses, and brays. At last, a human voice!

"I'm from Omsk," she said.

"Omsk?! My mama's from Omsk! I knew you were too pretty to be from Brooklyn . . . a little Siberian raven. What street did you live on? Where did you go to school?"

Anushka told him.

"That's the same neighborhood my mama grew up in! She'll want to meet you. I bet she knows your mama. What brings you to America?"

After two months of jury-rigged, lonesome English, the exquisite unthinking headiness of speaking Russian was like a shot of truth serum. Anushka couldn't stop talking, even when Ashley told her to shut up. Anushka told the wolverine how she'd come to New York to be an au pair for a theater agent's little boy, but was treated like a slave. Her employer hid spy cameras in the baby's toys and then threw Anushka out on the street with no money. She temporarily became an actress's roommate, but the actress kept her apartment so dirty that mushrooms grew in the closets.

"You're safe now," said the wolverine. "My mama will take care of you. She makes the best pierogies in Brighton Beach."

He reached into his sausage-tight pants pocket, removed a business card from his thick wallet, and wrote down his mother's address. The card was in Russian and English, embossed gold letters on slick white stock. He was in the import-export trade. Though the hour was four a.m., he told her he had to hop off at the next station to meet a business acquaintance—his deals ran on Moscow time—but afterward, he would meet Anushka at his mother's.

After he left, Anushka slipped his mother's address into her pocket to keep safe beside the gift card, but the gift card was gone.

Ashley was certain the wolverine had filched it, but Anushka still held out hope that someone's mama would take her in. She decided to get off at the Brighton Beach station and see if the address was real. Maybe a light would be on?

The train had risen above ground, two stories high. When she stepped onto the platform, she saw right into people's windows—a man's hairy arm in lamplight, a cat's arched shadow on a broken blind.

The address turned out to be a fish store.

She could smell and hear the ocean nearby. She'd never smelled or heard the ocean before. Under a moonless sky, the boardwalk was lit with old-fashioned globe lamps, but the world ended where the ocean began. Ashley crossed the sand and dipped her toe into the liquid black. Infinity splashed over her feet and lapped around her ankles. Infinity was surprisingly warm, not as warm as human blood, but warm enough to run through some beast's veins. She walked back to the brightly lit boardwalk and crawled underneath. The sand was cool and soft. She sensed she wasn't alone. Two black and orange tigers slept less than forty feet away. As silently as possible, Ashley burrowed her way into the sand until she was nearly invisible, and then kept vigilant watch over her pillowcase. In the first spark of dawn, the tigers turned into a sleeping old couple wearing identical orange jumpsuits. The stripes were the boardwalk's shadows.

Ashley shook off her sand blanket and crawled out to watch the sun rise over the ocean. Dawn was her favorite time of day. Sunrise made no promises. A bright young beginning didn't necessarily foretell a glorious evening, nor did a dark and livid start mean a stormy afternoon.

She was surprised by the polished surface of the flat calm sea—she could almost ice-skate across its featureless emptiness, but where would she skate to? Omsk? Loneliness seared her throat, as if she'd knocked back a shot of acid, but Ashley wasn't afraid of loneliness, or of hunger or thirst. She was frightened of insignificance.

"The *Times* says all the outbreaks are genetically identical."

"Mushrooms have genes?"

"Don't call them outbreaks. They're the fruit of a single gigantic mushroom growing under Brooklyn."

"Why don't they kill it! If it was growing under Manhattan, you better believe the authorities would find a way to kill it."

"What authorities? No one's in charge."

"It can't be killed. The taproot must be a thousand feet deep."

"Do mushrooms have taproots?"

"What's a taproot?"

"Only a cold snap can kill it. It's a tropical fungus. It needs heat and humidity."

"One grew under Rio that was five square miles; thousands died but they were squatters so we didn't hear about it."

"What about the one growing under Hong Kong?"

"I told you it came from China. Made in China might as well be a skull and bones."

"I thought ours was a whole new strain."

"It's a mutant."

"How did it cross the East River?"

"The Manhattan outbreaks are from a single carrier of

spores, that actress from the Ziberax commercial, Mushroom Mary. Every place she visits is followed by an outbreak."

"What about that building on Fifth and Forty-Second Street, the ghostscraper?"

Kat recognized Sutton House's address. Thank god she'd burned those letters. She sat cross-legged on her cot, finishing her breakfast of cold cereal and coffee, listening to the low dribble of rumors bouncing around the basketball court.

"Let's all get down on our knees and pray for the first frost."

"You think a cold snap will kill it? Ha! When hell freezes over."

That afternoon, bringing up the rear in a fresh line of new evacuees, Frank arrived.

"Frank! Oh, Frank!" Kat shouted.

His orange jumpsuit was a size too small. He must have endured the chemical showers. His face was brick red and sun-fried from the heat. His thirst must have been screaming, yet he ignored the volunteer passing out water bottles. He walked straight over to Kat and gave her a hug.

They sat side by side on her cot. He drank the sixteen-ounce water bottle that she brought him without taking a breath. His Adam's apple bobbed like a cork. His leg twitched from dehydration. Kat gently rested her hand on his knee. She felt the muscles still. Frank looked at her with gratitude, but he didn't stop drinking. In his too-tight jumpsuit, the solidity of his body made Kat feel rooted after so many itinerant days.

"The glow was so bright, it woke me. I thought my cousin left the bathroom light on," he told her after finally quenching his voracious thirst. She didn't retrieve her hand, though his leg was now as still as a tree trunk. "So I get up to see. My cousin's got one of those old claw-foot baths. It almost looked beautiful, like the tub was sculpted out of glowing ice. Then Annie, that's my cousin's wife, sees the slime and mushrooms and lets out a shriek. I'm deaf in one ear from my boxing days, but that shriek cured it. My cousin says we better keep this a secret or we'll be out on the street. I tell him I know people who died. He says him and me will remove the infested tub tonight, then rent a truck, and dump it somewhere. His wife goes nuts. Call the fire department, call the police! It's a plague from God! She takes her kids and goes to her sister's. Me and my cousin stay. We get the tub into the backyard and hide it under a tarp. Then he starts removing the bathroom floor, then the subfloor. It's like a glowing icicle had been bored deep into the basement. It's the root, I tell him. But he doesn't listen. He tries to dig it out. Maybe hell is made of ice, Kat, not fire. Turns out one of his neighbors reports a suspicious glow under a tarp in the backyard, and here I am."

"I'm so glad you're here," Kat said after he had slaked his thirst for talking. She told him how she had to destroy the letters she'd hoped to publish as a tribute to Edith and her mother. "It felt like I was burning history, but what choice did I have? The pages were alive, Frank. They didn't smell like paper burning, they smelled like scorched flesh."

The whole time she spoke, Frank comforted her and stroked her hand, the one still on his knee, with his big-knuckled, clay-warm fingers. The weight of his touch felt unexpectedly fragile to Kat, as if the hand had long ago been shattered, and then reassembled with a piece or two absent, like an ancient vase glued together with bits missing.

. . .

Just before dinner, a Red Cross volunteer handed Kate one of the shelter's public cell phones.

"Katherine, it's Stanley Flom. I've been trying to reach you for days. I left messages on Edith's voicemail."

"That number is no longer in service," Kat said.

"I wanted to let you know that Edith's body is finally being released. I'm afraid the Jewish funeral home we chose can no longer accept her. Her remains have been classified as biohazardous. Her body is required by law to be cremated at a facility with provisions for hazardous waste. There's a facility in the Bronx, I'm told."

"A funeral home or just an incinerator?"

"Janice—you remember my secretary—looked up the mortuary online and said it was quite dignified. There was a picture of a lovely chapel."

"Will she have a casket?"

"I believe so. Do you want to pick one out?"

"I don't care as long as it's not a biohazard bag."

Gladys found Kat a black dress and navy shoes in one of the donated boxes of clothes. Frank claimed a dark jacket and tie from the men's selection. Mr. and Mrs. Syzmanski drove everyone to the service. The Syzmanskis still had their car. The crematorium was a windowless freestanding building in an industrial Bronx neighborhood. If not for the smokestack out back, Kat would have guessed they were lost.

The funeral director escorted them into the chapel. Thirty-odd folding chairs had been set up. The pine casket, on wheels, faced a heavy theatrical black drape. Feetfirst or headfirst? Edith was afraid of diving. She always plunged feetfirst into the water, as if a rug had been pulled out from under her. To think her sister was in that box.

An expensive black rose wreath had been laid over the casket's lid. Stanley and Janice occupied the second row, dressed for work, not sorrow, as if they were only taking a half day off, though Janice was openly weeping. Edith's wishes stipulated no clergy, so the funeral director held a moment of silence before trundling the casket through the drapes. Kat caught a glimpse of what awaited her on the other side—not a brick incinerator as she'd imagined, but a stainless steel oven. She hoped Edith was feetfirst. She closed her eyes, but she only saw more clearly—a conflagration vibrant and alive, performing a sinuous dance over her sister's flesh.

At the small reception afterward, while Frank brought her a cup of coffee, Kat looked around for Vida. Price, Bloodworth had taken out a death announcement in the *Times*. Kat thought maybe Vida would pay her respects after what happened.

"She's not coming," said Frank, eating a Danish. "She wouldn't dare show her face after what she did to Edith. You see her YouTube video yet?"

Frank unholstered his phone and called up Vida's video. He kept the volume low out of respect for Edith. How could Kat not be curious? When the side effects were read at the end, the grief fermenting within her for the past two weeks escaped as burps of laughter. Stanley and Janice looked at her as if the wrong twin had died.

PART TWO

TILL KINGDOM COME

When a mid-October cold snap stopped the outbreaks, the *New York Post* ran the last of three infestation headlines—*GIANT KILLER MUSHROOM ATTACKS BROOKLYN! GUESS WHO MUSHROOM MARY IS? SHROOM-AGEDDON V-DAY.* Vida's YouTube video now garnered less than a handful of hits daily and Jay Leno's joke—*How many Ziberax ladies does it take to screw in a light bulb? None, they already glow in the dark*—was all but forgotten.

Maybe now she could finally get back to her work. The hardest part of acting was not acting.

She'd been living with Virginia in the maid's room off the kitchen, vacated three months ago by Zachary's Russian au pair. The second night after Vida moved in, Virginia regaled her with the whole Slav saga, reddening in capillary rage as she played Vida a poor-quality security video of a birdlike, black-haired girl feeding something tiny and white to Zachary. Had Virginia shown her the video before? The girl looked uncannily familiar. Virginia planned to install a new au pair in the narrow back room, a demure Midwestern girl this time instead of a Slavic sociopath, as soon as Vida found her own place. But instead of industriously seeking lodgings, Vida doggedly hunted for roles, calling everyone she knew in the business, without telling Virginia.

The third week of her stay, Zachary woke up with a fever

and couldn't go to day care. Virginia asked Vida to babysit, just this one time. One time turned into five straight days. Performing broad comedy to entertain a sick toddler wasn't the role she was seeking. When the boxy, coarse-haired Zachary grew tired of her funny faces, he butted his head, like a kid goat, against the crib bars and screamed in anger or boredom, she couldn't distinguish. She tried to soothe him and tell him his mommy was coming home *not soon enough,* but his eerily sentient black eyes didn't believe her. He released a banshee war cry. Vida understood why the Russian had slipped him the occasional Ambien. Her friendship with Virginia had withstood the trespass and tussle of working together, agent and actress, but Vida doubted their friendship would survive one more day if she had to babysit Zachary any longer.

All her savings, which were never much, and all the money she made on the Ziberax ad, an indecent amount considering the effort, had been shoveled into the charred pit on Berry Street. The renovations had cost twice the estimate. Her credit cards were sodden with debt; they couldn't absorb more. She had eight grand in the bank, the final payment before Pfizer pulled the commercial. Eight thousand would scarcely cover first, last, security deposit, and broker fee. She'd have to settle for a roommate. She limited her search to Brooklyn and found Jodie, a twentysomething aspiring actress with a twelve-hundred-a-month furnished share near the Williamsburg Bridge. To avoid spending evenings in the apartment while Jodie earnestly practiced for acting class, Vida worked out at her gym, fervently, as she nightly attempted to climb all the way to heaven on a StairMaster. To get to the gym from Jodie's she had to pass through her disfigured neighborhood. Fatality and plain vanilla homesickness invariably drew her to her front door, now a gaping cavity in a black tooth. Abandoned for less than three months, her house was a ruin—one wall had crumbled, a couple of roof joists now hung diagonally; all the picture lacked were weeds and roosting pigeons. But nothing grew or nested in the ten square blocks of no-man's-land. The few lucky intact houses that had survived the plague didn't look so lucky now. Cars and taxis avoided the ash-heaped streets mined with broken glass and other tire-popping debris. Even parking-starved New Yorkers didn't take advantage of the vacant spots.

One evening, a beige sedan pulled onto her block and stopped. Whoever was driving cut the engine and doused the headlights, but didn't get out. The car's interior light came on. Vida recognized the old Polish couple from down the street. Mr. Syzmanski was behind the wheel. Beside him, his short wife's dread-filled eyes peeked over the dashboard. Vida waved to her former neighbors, but they didn't appear to see her in the twilight, against a charcoal-black set. She was curious to see how others approached fate's fist to the jaw and then managed the operations of normal life—opening a car door, marching up the stoop steps. But the old couple chose not to march up to the abyss's edge. They remained in their sedan, doors locked, fearful and immobilized, staring through the windshield, as if waiting for a drive-in horror movie to end. Vida watched as Mr. Syzmanski reached over to cover his wife's eyes.

That night, a Help sign for a receptionist was posted on the gym door. Vida stopped by the empty front desk and called for Jimmy, the gym's bull-necked, flirtatious owner. He and Vida had slept together a few times for sport. When she asked for the job, he thought she was kidding.

"I wish I were," she said.

The fall from Queen Goneril to receptionist and towel

girl had all the makings of a tragedy, but her other possible role, a middle-aged unemployed actress seeking work with no marketable skills unless crying-on-cue counts, had all the makings of a farce. Most of the gym's clientele recognized her, if not as the infamous Mushroom Mary, aka Ziberax Lady, then as a fellow gym member, and when she fetched a towel or answered the phone, some kindly averted their eyes and pretended not to see, some attached themselves to her and tried to feed off her bad luck, some offered samplings of pop psychology, some offered condolences, some secretly gloated, but worst of all were the other gym members from no-man's-land now sleeping on friends' sofas or in cars, the rumpled glassy-eyed refugees who arrived first thing in the morning to shower before work. They recognized her as one of their own.

After the night she saw the Syzmanskis, she avoided her old street on the way home from work. But the couple remained on her mind. She couldn't shake the image of Mr. Syzmanski reaching across the sedan's front seat to cover his wife's eyes. Vida had never felt more alone than in these past months, and not because she wasn't involved with anyone. She'd never gone this long without a role to keep her company. She had gladly put off marriage and children for her acting, but until now, she hadn't realized that she'd also put off the possibility of having someone's loving hand cover her eyes when she was scared.

She walked by the high school where the last of the evacuees still remained, those without family or the means to move on. Outside the gymnasium door, under the glow of an exit light, two people kissed. Vida found it remarkable that love could survive under such conditions. She could tell the kiss wasn't just carnal, although it was that, too. It was tender and romantic. The couple braided into a singular shape. When the kiss finally ended and the couple parted, she recognized Frank and Kat.

Nightly, Frank broke the shelter rule of separating single men after lights-out and slipped into Kat's cot. They kissed and caressed a little under the covers, but they couldn't really lose themselves. Inches away, Mrs. Syzmanski did needle-point by flashlight.

Usually, they watched a movie on Frank's phone, but tonight Kat needed to talk. "Tomorrow is Edith's and my birthday. I think about her more and more, Frank, not less. I don't know how to be without her. I'm still a twin—a twin-less twin. I'd bring her back if I could, but as ashamed as I am to say it, I also feel free in a way I never have before. I was born married, engaged for nine months before that. All my life, Edith was my other self, the choices I didn't make, or maybe I was the choices she didn't make, as if we were part of a double-blind medical study, only we didn't know which one got the real medicine and which one the sugar pill. I feel horribly guilty taking any pleasure in her death."

"She loved you. She always said Kat doesn't see the glass as half full, she sees it as overflowing."

"Remember that lawyer, Stanley, who was at the funeral? I think his wife may have been Edith's lover. Edith tried to tell me a story once about a partner's wife, the 'most charm-ing woman,' she called her, and I cut her short, and said something like, 'Edie, please, for your own good, get a life outside the office or you'll have no life.' Why didn't I listen to her? Why didn't she just tell me?"

"Edith knew you don't got a judgmental bone in your body. She was a grown-up lady living with her mother. She probably needed a secret."

"She left me some money, Frank."

"So how come you live at a shelter?"

"She set it up so that I couldn't touch a penny until our sixty-fifth birthday. I don't think there's much, Frank, but I'll find out tomorrow."

His face knit together with hurt and bewilderment. "You knew about the money all along and you never told me?"

"I was embarrassed. My own sister didn't trust me enough to manage my money, let alone hers. And maybe she was right."

"I can't believe she never told you how much."

"She never even told me about Alice."

Kat sat across from Stanley in his vast spotless office, a view of Madison Square framing his domed head. Janice had brought in a tray of coffee with real cream and old-fashioned sugar cubes. A check lay shockingly white on his black leather desk pad, too far away for her to see the amount.

"Today must be a difficult birthday for you without her," he said kindly. "This shouldn't take long."

After signing the stack of legal documents he set before her, she waited for him to stand ceremoniously and shake her hand before giving her the check, fifty-eight hundred dollars. She put it in her purse. Why did she feel like she was stealing it?

"Well, Kat, you'll be able to get your own place now.

Janice will help you set up a bank account. The trust can do direct deposits, unless you prefer that the checks be mailed to your new place?"

"There are more?"

"Yes. The first of every month."

While the bank teller counted out her money—fifty twenties, twenty fifties, and thirty-eight hundred-dollar bills—Kat's emotions ran from elation to disbelief to gratitude to hurt. Why had Edith thought it necessary to hide the fact that she was rich?

One more secret.

Outside the bank, on the bustling avenue, Kat couldn't help but feel exuberant with the weight of those bills in her purse. She hailed a taxi. The whole drive back to Brooklyn, she planned a surprise for Frank. She'd take him to an expensive dinner and then book them into a nice hotel, maybe someplace on Central Park. Or maybe instead of a restaurant, they should order room service with iced Champagne? A honeymoon.

As the taxi crossed over the Williamsburg Bridge, she got her first bird's-eye view of her old neighborhood. From this vantage point, the devastation didn't look as large as she had imagined. Yes, the burnt-out row houses were a travesty, but it was only ten square blocks in an otherwise thriving borough. A subway car rattled past the stalled bridge traffic. No one inside bothered to look out the window.

She considered asking the cabbie to wait outside while she ran in and got Frank, but as they approached the school, she had him drive past and drop her off a block away. She hadn't realized until now how difficult it would be to tell Gladys and Mrs. Syzmanski, practically family at this point, that she and Frank were moving on. She knew they would be happy for them, but in the end, how could they not feel forgotten? No matter how she couched it, all that they would hear was *Good-bye and good luck.*

When she opened the gym's double doors, she heard a commotion coming from her quadrant of cots. Mr. Syzmanski, an ox-stout, dome-bellied man who usually sat mutely all day, was stomping and kicking his cot, as if he were trying to kill it.

"You'll break your foot, you crazy old man," yelled Mrs. Syzmanski.

The shelter's security guard hurried over, but Frank got to the old man first. She couldn't hear what Frank whispered to him, but she watched as the rage deflated in Mr. Syzmanski's domed belly until he looked almost concave. Mrs. Syzmanski clutched the big gold cross yoking her double chin and watched with grave, anxious eyes as Frank led her husband outside for fresh air.

"The shelter is closing next week," she told Kat. "We're getting vouchers to a motel in Yonkers, but he said he'd rather live in our car. We're going to freeze to death in our car."

"The motel doesn't take pets. I can't move to another place that won't take my babies," said Gladys.

"As soon as that fuckball insurance company pays what's owed me, I'm rebuilding. 'Act of god' my fucking asshole!" yelled Marty.

"How are we supposed to rebuild from Yonkers?" a gruff voice on the far side of the gym shouted.

"Can't we get FEMA trailers like they had in New Orleans and park them next to our houses?" asked a single mother with two hyperactive boys.

"You want we should live in a FEMA trailer?" a raspy older voice answered. "Those trailers were toxic. The formaldehyde made the people of New Orleans sicker than the debris."

Mrs. Syzmanski searched Kat's face. "I used to go to Edith for advice when he acted crazy like this. Your sister was such a wise lady. I called her Dr. Edie after your mother, everyone did." She graced her lips with her cross. "Maybe you can help me now? He says to me, 'I'm going to kill myself.' He wants us to go to sleep in our car and never wake up. He says, 'Freezing to death is supposed to be a good way to die.' Should I tell one of the social workers? I'm worried they'll take him away and commit him. Then where I will go?"

What was Kat supposed to say? Who was she to give advice?

She opened her purse's jaws wide, and showed the astonished Mrs. Syzmanski and the weepy Gladys the brick of cash.

"Edith wanted us all to share this."

Mrs. Syzmanski shook her head in wonder. "How much is there?" she whispered.

"Enough so that no one has to move to Yonkers."

Gladys kissed her hand. "Thank you, Edith."

Tomorrow, she and Frank would look for a place to rent, big enough for all, or three smaller apartments near one another, but tonight she was taking him to a hotel. She could no longer splurge on a park view if she was to make good on her promise, but she found them a nice two-star near the river.

Alone in a room at last, they had their first unabashed kiss. She remembered what a good kisser he'd been, but she didn't kiss him wildly back, as she had forty years ago. She felt inexplicably bashful. Their circumstances had created a courtship and she had never been courted before. She'd always been too eager for adventure to delay sex. Was that the source of her shyness? Or was it because Frank hadn't seen her naked in forty years? As he undressed her, reaching under her sweater to touch her breasts, her shyness became exquisitely painful. Here she was, sixty-five years old and gray—she hadn't dyed her hair in months—and in love for the first time. She'd always believed she'd been in love before, countless times. She'd certainly known zealous passion and fanatical lust, but she'd never known shyness, not like this.

Afterward, Frank looked at her as if she might not be real. "I always thought you were the prettier sister."

Ashley felt the cold snap as Siberian teeth. Though she marveled to see her arctic-white skin burnished to bronze, her time at the beach had hardly been a holiday. She'd been forced to eat half-finished hamburgers left for the gulls, ketchup packets stolen from Coney Island hot dog stands. She filched anything left unguarded on a beach towel, and sometimes she stole the towel, too.

There were mornings when hunger was her only company, days when anguish choked her like a fish bone. Hearing Russian being spoken on the boardwalk only made the bone prick sharper. Some evenings, just as twilight leeched every color from the world and the phantasmagoric gyrating lights of Coney Island's colossal Wonder Wheel blinked on, Ashley considered swimming out into black infinity. Maybe home was on the other side? To be alone and unloved in such a beautiful alien land.

Once the temperature dropped, she knew she needed sounder shelter than an encampment under the boardwalk. She migrated back to the old neighborhood by the river and moved into a parked car with a busted door lock and a theft-proof gadget on the steering wheel. Once she got the hang of alternate-side-of-the-street parking, she knew exactly when to move her encampment in and out—a beach blanket, four iPods, three watches, two wallets, and a purse with all sorts of makeup. Aside from moving the car for the street sweeper twice a week, the scruffy, unshaven owner of the car never drove anywhere. If she had the keys, she'd light out for California, or maybe Florida. She could learn to drive on the fly. She'd fire up her four iPods with the cigarette lighter, and let them serenade her all the way to Hollywood, or maybe South Beach. For food, she'd rob gas station concession stands. She had a getaway car. When she got sick of pretzels and cola, she'd eat at diners, steaks and potatoes and hot dogs and ice cream, and then sneak out a bathroom window. She almost tasted the meat as she lay curled on the hatchback's rear seat, the beach blanket pulled up to her chin for warmth.

Just as she dozed off, a fist commenced pounding on the window. The car owner's unshaven face, lit by a streetlight, contorted and snarled behind the glass. "What the fuck!"

When she sat up and he saw that she was female, and tiny, and very pretty, his expression switched from belligerent to disbelieving.

"I scream rape if you call police," Ashley threatened as he opened the door with his key.

"I'm not going to hurt you," he said, holding his hands wide and taking a giant step back. "But you can't sleep here."

"So? I be car's guard. Lock broken. You go nowhere anyway."

He looked over the front seat headrest to her encampment below—the watches and purse and iPods.

"How long have you been here?"

"Why? You have weekly rate?"

"I need to use the car. You need to leave. Now."

"Where going? Maybe I come."

"I'm going to my girlfriend's house upstate. It's her car."

Ashley packed her belongings like checkout time wasn't

till noon. She dreaded going outside. The night air was blustery. All she had to keep warm was the beach blanket. She walked for blocks jiggling car door handles to see if one would open. Outside a grocery store, she stopped to calculate the risk of stealing dinner when she spotted Edith, the sister that Kat had told her was dead. Why would Kat have said she was dead? Probably to trick her into feeling sorry for her so that she would give Kat back the letters. Kat had only pretended to be her friend. The stout, gray-haired twin was paying for eight large bags of groceries when Vida's super walked up to her at the register with one last item to buy, the wrapper of a chocolate bar he was finishing. She smiled at him. Even from twenty feet away, looking through a frosted shop window, Ashley recognized Kat's big false teeth.

Keeping twenty paces behind, she followed them to a three-story clapboard house with steamy windows. Six cat silhouettes slept on the sills. It must be warm inside.

She stepped out of the shadows. "You still need Russian translator?"

"Give us a minute, Frank," Kat told the super, who hauled in all eight bags of food, then shut the door with his foot.

Ashley felt hunger twist her intestines, like a bully twists a weakling's arm.

"Why should I even talk to you?" Kat asked.

"I translate for food."

"There's nothing left to translate, Ashley. I had to burn the letters."

"I sorry I steal gift card," she said, casting her eyes down in contrition, though all she really felt was ravenousness.

"You were supposed to be my friend."

"I punished. Man rob card from me anyway."

"I would have shared the money," Kat said, opening the

door wide enough for Ashley and her stuffed pillowcase to fit through. "Come on in, you look like you could use a hot meal."

Once the warmth kissed her skin, she began shivering. The house smelled of cabbage and sausages. An old Polish woman was making dinner in the kitchen. Kat went to get her a cup of hot tea and a snack to hold her over until dinner. Alone in the living room, she wandered around. The walls smelled of fresh paint. The furniture looked new. The shelves had nothing on them, no photographs or knick-knacks. When Kat returned, Ashley ate the bread and cheese so fast she forgot to taste it and drank the tea before it cooled, scalding her lips and tongue.

"You look skinny, Ashley. Where have you been?"

"God punish me big-time. I eat only ketchup and garbage. I live under boardwalk, like rat."

"You lived on the beach?"

"First time see ocean."

"Your first time? You'd never seen the ocean before? Oh, Ashley, the first time is primal."

"No big deal," Ashley said, but it wasn't true. The first time she'd dipped her toe into the sea and felt its volatility and vastness, she realized all humans were *insignificuntskis,* but rather than that knowledge diminishing her, it made her less lonely.

"It must have been scary living under the boardwalk," Kat said. "I know. I once had to sleep in a doorway."

"I never scared."

"Everybody is scared, Ashley. I'm scared something will happen to Frank. I'm scared whatever killed Edith is inside me. I'm scared my happiness will end."

"Okay, maybe I scared a little."

"Of what?"

She didn't know how to translate *insignificuntski,* so she put it another way: "I scared I end back in Omsk."

"Would that be so bad? Your parents are probably worried sick."

"Probably sold bed day I go."

"I ran off at your age. You can't imagine how I worried my mother and Edith when I dropped out of college to follow the Grateful Dead."

American dead are grateful? "You follow dead people?"

"It was the name of a band. The point is you shouldn't follow anyone but yourself. That was my mistake. You can do and be anyone you want."

"Lady Gaga?"

"How about Ashley? After all, she didn't exist until you made her up."

Dinner was served in the kitchen, a communal bowl steaming on a table set for six. After Kat introduced her to everyone, Ashley sat on the only empty chair, at the table's far end. Whenever her mother set a bowl of food before her and her siblings, eight forks clashed to get at the one piece of meat. With practiced adroitness, Ashley speared the largest sausage for herself before anyone else had a chance to pick up his fork. Only after she'd devoured half of it did she look up and see that the others were gaping at her, as if she were a wild animal.

"It's been a while since Ashley had a home-cooked meal," said Kat, breaking the silence by spearing an ample sausage herself.

"Guess who I saw yesterday?" said the lady with a black cat on her lap.

"Vida," guessed the Polish cook. "Word is she's working at a nearby gym."

"Someone hired Mushroom Mary to work with the public?" asked her husband.

"Jimmy, the guy who owns the gym, told me she had to declare bankruptcy," said Frank.

"I know I shouldn't torture myself," said Kat, "but sometimes I wonder how different it might have been if only she'd listened to Edith in time, but she claims she never heard Edith's messages."

"She heard them," said Frank. "She's an actress. Who ever heard of an actress not listening to her messages?"

"She says Edith's death was nobody's fault. An 'act of God,' she called it."

Ashley ached to be part of the camaraderie, but no one paid attention to her. Her stomach was full, but she didn't feel any less lonely in this warm kitchen than she did under the boardwalk. She speared a second sausage. Didn't Kat promise her she could be anyone she wanted?

"I Vida's houseguest," she announced. "I there when mushroom found. I see Vida listen to messages. I hear Edith say something smell funny in basement." In fact, hiding in Vida's guest room closet, she'd heard nothing except her own pulse.

But she had everyone's attention now.

"You saw her and you never told me?" asked Kat.

"I tell you now. She laugh when Edith leave message."

"She laughed?" Kat looked as surprised as pained.

That night Ashley slept in a room on the ground floor, across from the Polish couple's door. Other than a bed, the only decor was an empty bureau and wire hangers in the closet. Kat had promised to buy her a new winter coat and boots tomorrow. She opened her pillowcase and removed the plastic laptop she'd been hauling around since her penthouse days. She set it on the bureau and squared it so that it sat dead center. Then she hung up the few rags she owned on the wire hangers.

She crawled under the covers. She hadn't felt this safe and warm in weeks, but rather than it relaxing her, it made her more anxious. She looked at the moon through her curtainless window, the same moon she had slept under at the beach. She heard scratching at her door. She opened it, a cat slipped in. She tried to chase it out, but it hid under the bureau. She got back in bed, and the cat joined her. It settled on her chest, emitting a low-pitched vibrato, a feline lullaby that soothed her to sleep.

"Should I believe that girl?" Kat asked Frank as they got into bed that evening. Their room was on the third floor with a sitting area and a private bath. "I think she was so desperate to stay the night that she would have said or done anything. When I invited her in earlier, I wondered if I wasn't inviting trouble. She stole from me, Frank, my last hundred dollars. But she looked so lost standing under the streetlight. Yes, she looked skinny and hungry and cold, too, but basically, she looked lonely. I wonder if I used to look that way to Edith when I just showed up uninvited at her door?"

She propped herself up on her elbow. Frank's eyes were closed, but she knew he was listening. "You think Vida is evil like Gladys and Mrs. Syzmanski called her tonight?"

"Mrs. Syzmanski goes to Mass every morning and Gladys lights votive candles for her dead cats. They only know from good and evil."

"You believe it was an act of God, Frank?"

"I used to get on my knees before every fight and pray for God to let me knock the lights out of my opponent. You know how God answered? He knocked out one of my lights." He pointed to his blind one. "I say to hell with God."

"You think Vida is responsible for Edith's death?"

"I don't know if God or the oil spill or the Chinese wall-board brought the supermold, but no matter, Vida should of returned Edith's calls right away. She owes you an apology. Maybe she owes us all an apology."

"Can you legally make someone apologize?" Kat asked Stanley over the phone the next morning after she explained to him how her former landlady had contributed to Edith's death.

"I don't want to be discouraging, Katherine, but a wrongful death suit can drag on for years. In the end, the only ones to get rich are the lawyers."

"It's not about the money. I just want an apology."

"An apology is an admission of guilt, and her insurance company might not like that. If human negligence contributed in any way to the infestation, they could be out tens of millions. They have a vested interest in proving that the mold was an act of God."

"Maybe the mold was an act of God, but Edith's death wasn't. She might have gotten out in time if only Vida had listened to her."

"Have you tried just asking her for an apology?"

"She claims she never heard the warnings Edith left on her answering machine, but I don't believe her."

"If you're sure about forgoing monetary damages and all you're seeking is an apology, there's a fairly modern trend these days called 'restorative justice.' It's not a litigious procedure so the insurance company needn't get involved. But it is a legal action. The offender—in this case your landlady—must go on public record to take full responsibility for his or her wrongdoings and offer an apology. It seems to give the victims a sense of fairness and closure."

"Would I have to forgive her?"

"That would be entirely up to you."

"Consider yourself served," said the stocky leather-clad man waiting for Vida outside the gym at six a.m. Mystified, Vida accepted the envelope as the man took off on a motorcycle.

Before breaking the seal, she read the name on the return address: Price, Bloodworth, Flom, Mead & Van Doren, LLC. She'd never heard of the law firm, but those names alone sounded foreboding.

Dear Ms. Vida Cebu,

This letter concerns the unfortunate death of Edith Glasser from an ischemic stroke caused by fungal pneumonia contracted during her lawful residence in your apartment building. My client and the sister of the deceased, Katherine Glasser, is prepared to forgo a lawsuit seeking damages on the condition that you acknowledge your role in failing to take reasonable and practical measures to mitigate the damage that the infestation of toxic mold was causing to the well-being of the occupants. The pathology report leaves no room for doubt that inhalation of spoor was the principal factor in her death. In lieu of a lawsuit for damages and in release of all claims against you for wrongful death, my client seeks a written apology.

This apology must demonstrate to my client your acknowledgment of culpability and your heartfelt regret for failing to take action. Failure to provide this written apology within fourteen days of the receipt of this letter will result in a revocation of the offer and litigation will commence soon after.

I strongly urge you to review this letter with your own counsel.

Sincerely,
Stanley Flom
Senior Partner

After she opened the gym, she called Virginia. "What do you make of this?"

"Vida, I haven't practiced law in ten years."

"Maybe I should just go ahead and apologize. The poor woman lost her twin sister."

"The question is what exactly are you apologizing for? Or more to the point, what does she imagine you're apologizing for?"

"That I didn't find out about the mold in time. Her sister called me to complain about a smell in the basement and I didn't return her call right away. It was the same week I had that squatter camping in my guest room closet. By the time I was shown the first mushroom by the police, it was too late to do anything. I had to flee with only the clothes on my back, too."

"Why don't you explain that to her? Don't admit to any blame, but make sure your condolences sound heartfelt. Maybe she just needs someone to say they're sorry for her sister's death. A twin, it must be so hard. Just make sure you read me the letter beforehand."

The gym began filling up with regulars. The first to arrive every morning was an intense young man slathered in Bengay; then came the breast-augmented hedge fund manager who walked the treadmill while shouting into her cell as if her voice had to carry twelve thousand miles on its own power to reach her partner in Hong Kong; then came the saddest client of all, the chubby boy who never seemed to lose weight. His routine consisted solely of squats.

No actor can make a life's work out of self-exhibition without some colossal need to be noticed. Vida's morning workout, if you will, was to exercise a kind of hypnotic power over one of the regulars and get them to look up and notice her without her doing anything to attract their attention. It wasn't acting, but it was as close as this job got.

The chubby boy was grunting at his mirrored reflection, his broad back to her. He was easily crunching two hundred and fifty pounds, the canyon between his buttocks widening with each squat. Vida exerted her powers and he spun around, as if a ghost had tapped him on the shoulder. His look of despondency caught her off guard. Whatever demons he was crunching weighed a lot more than two hundred and fifty pounds.

That night she sat down to compose her apology with pen and ink. A handwritten letter seemed the only appropriate way to convey true sorrow, and she felt awful about Edith's death. But every draft ended up in the wastepaper basket. She couldn't find the right tone. Should she begin with the apology or the explanation? When she started with the apology, the explanation read like a proviso on her sorrow. When she began with the explanation, the apology sounded like an afterthought.

Halfway through the fourth attempt she finally realized why. She wasn't telling the whole truth. The morning that Edith had left the first message about the smell was the same day she had had lunch with her old mentor, eighty-nine and still producing. He'd started in burlesque and never minced words. When she complained to him that no one was considering her for any good parts, he told her point-blank why. "You're the Ziberax lady. Who wants the media circus your name will bring to a serious project?"

When she came home that afternoon and heard Edith's voice on her answering machine, she pressed the Erase button. Edith was always complaining about something, and Vida didn't have the wherewithal to listen to another lecture on building maintenance when her career was dying.

She put down the pen and went to the mirror. If she could act out the apology, maybe she'd find the right tone. Her mouth frowned and her eyes filled with tears. She had captured sorrow, but what did repentance look like? She mentally skimmed the pages of Darwin's *The Expression of the Emotions in Man and Animals,* but she couldn't recall repentance. He must not have included it.

Of course he hadn't included it. Animals don't repent.

Dear Katherine,

Please know how deeply sorry I am about Edith's passing. She was beloved by everyone who knew her and her loss is a tragedy. Had I known she was in danger prior to us all being evacuated I would have taken immediate action.

I never heard Edith's messages. I never had the

chance. There was an intruder in my house. I only found out about the mold after the police arrived to arrest her. One of the officers found a mushroom in the closet where she'd been hiding.

Katherine, I can't begin to imagine how difficult and devastating it is to lose a sister, a twin sister. My heart goes out to you.

Sincerely yours,
Vida

Kat read the letter with raw disappointment. "Where is the apology? She takes no responsibility."

Frank read it with simmering deliberation. "Vida knew about the smell before she called the police on Ashley. She told me to check the basement for leaks."

They sat on matching armchairs in Stanley's corner office. He'd stepped outside to give them privacy. This morning, when he had called to tell her that Vida's letter had arrived, she'd told Frank that all she wanted was finality and peace. She felt anything but peaceful now.

"She blames Ashley, Frank. What does a ninety-pound scared girl hiding in a closet have to do with her not calling Edith back?"

"Tell her to go to hell. She listened to Edith's messages."

"My god, all she has to say is 'I'm sorry I didn't call Edith back.'"

"Tear up the letter and mail her back the pieces."

"And then what? Make good on my threat? Stanley said a lawsuit could last years. It will only be a constant reminder that I've lost Edie."

"Tell her she's got to write you another letter."

"It will only be another chance for her to make excuses."

"Spell out what you want her to say."

"I want her to look me in the eye and say, 'I'm sorry I didn't call Edith back.'"

Dear Ms. Vida Cebu,

My client, Katherine Glasser, found your letter of apology woefully inadequate and is offended by what she considers to be your obstinate avoidance of accepting responsibility for not returning the deceased's calls with prudent expediency. She wants you to take the remainder of the fourteen-day deadline to reflect on how your actions as the property owner, responsible for her tenants' health, contributed to the premature death of Edith Glasser. My client loved her sister very much and is devastated by her death. She wants closure to this tragic situation.

The offer to forgo monetary damages will expire unless you appear in person at my offices on March 19 prepared to admit culpability and offer my grieving client a heartfelt and meaningful apology.

Sincerely,
Stanley Flom
Senior Partner

"Will you come with me?" Vida asked Virginia after reading her the letter over the phone. She sat in Jimmy's private office at the gym.

"Maybe you should get a real lawyer, Vid. You'll be under oath."

"Virginia, I'm honestly sorry that her sister is dead."

"What I meant to say is that the proceeding will be on public record and is open to anyone who wants to attend."

"Who do you expect to come?"

"What if the tabloids get wind of this?"

"Can't we ask that the proceeding be closed?"

"I don't think that's in the spirit of restorative justice."

" 'Ziberax Lady Apologizes for the Plague.' I'll never get another part."

"Vida, you're a great actress. You can convince her that you're telling the truth."

"I didn't realize we'd be in the library," Kat said to Stanley as he opened the mahogany doors. She'd never before seen where Edith had worked. Victorian glass-fronted bookshelves lined all four walls. Leather-bound tomes in muted colors were bricked ceiling high. The only way to reach the top volumes was a library ladder on tracks. How many times had Edith climbed those rungs? She felt as if she were entering the interior of her sister's soul.

"We don't really use the library anymore," he said, pulling out a chair for her at one end of a long conference table. "Everything's digital nowadays."

"Will Vida be under oath?" asked Kat.

"It's a legal proceeding, no different than if we held it in open court."

"What if she still contends she never heard Edith's messages?"

"We'll bring in your fiancé and niece to contest her version of events."

Back in Stanley's office, Frank and Ashley waited on the matching armchairs.

A few minutes later, before Kat had time to collect herself, Vida came through the heavy doors and walked to the conference table's opposite shore, accompanied by her counsel, a plump woman about Vida's age with a Botox-frozen expression. Vida hadn't lost weight, exactly, but she looked tinier to Kat, as if her skin had shrunk from the winter damp and now fit her like a tight leather glove. She must have been to hell and back too, thought Kat.

Stanley's assistant, a bow-tied young man, positioned a video camera and switched it on.

"I didn't agree to be filmed," Vida objected.

The bow-tied assistant shut the camera off and replaced it with an audio device, as thin as a playing card, while Janice appeared with a tray of coffee and some delicious-smelling pastries.

Only Vida's lawyer helped herself to a croissant.

After Janice left, Stanley asked everyone to state names and addresses for the record and then had Vida stand and raise her right hand.

"Ms. Cebu," he said when the oath was over, "my client is waiting for her apology."

"May I move closer? I don't want to have to shout."

"Do you have any objection, Katherine?"

"No."

Yet when Vida sat directly across from her, Kat instinctively moved her chair back an inch or two. She waited as Vida prepared to speak. Vida appeared to be measuring her breathing, a method she must have learned for the stage.

"Katherine, Edith's death was a terrible tragedy. I think about her every day. I wish I could turn back the clock and listen to her warnings in time to save her, but I can't. You've lost your sister, your twin. I accept all blame for any part I had in her death. I'm sorry I never had the chance to call her back. I'm sorry I didn't know about the mold's toxicity. I'm sorry, so deeply sorry for your loss."

"Why didn't you call her back?"

"I never had the chance, Kat. There was an intruder in my home."

"She left more than one message."

"The police arrived before I had a chance to play them."

"I don't believe you."

"My client would like to call her first witness," interjected Stanley.

"What witnesses?" asked Vida.

Frank came in looking especially handsome in his new dark gray suit and sat beside Kat. He didn't console her with a gentle touch: he'd been instructed not to. He unbuttoned his jacket and folded his hands on the conference table, like the obedient schoolboy he must have been. After he was sworn in, he could no longer resist the sugary display, though he took his time selecting a pastry.

Stanley asked, "What is your relationship to Ms. Cebu?"

"She was my boss. Last year she bought the apartment building I took care of for nearly forty years."

"On August eleventh, did you have a conversation with Ms. Cebu about a foul odor in her basement?"

"She said I should check the cellar for leaks because something smelled nasty down there."

"Did you then check the basement for leaks?"

"It was too late. The building got condemned."

Stanley thanked Frank for his testimony, and then asked Vida and her counsel if they had any questions for the witness.

"Yes," Vida's counsel said, brushing a flaky crumb off her sleeve. "At any time during the aforementioned date, did you witness, with your own eyes and ears, my client listening to Edith Glasser's phone messages?"

"She's an actress, course she listens to her phone messages."

"I'm not asking you to speculate. Were you inside Ms. Cebu's apartment on that date?"

"No."

"Thank you, no more questions."

"I have a witness who was inside the apartment," said Kat.

Yesterday she'd given Ashley money to buy something pretty but appropriate to wear to court this morning. Opening the library doors, Ashley appeared in her new red satin dress. She clacked loudly across the floor in her matching red platform heels. The little dress was so tight that Kat could almost see Ashley's heart beating.

"*She's* your witness?" gasped Vida's counsel. "She's a sociopathic liar. I brought her over from Russia to be part of my family and take care of my son. She drugged him with Ambien!"

"What does that have to do with my sister's death?"

"She should be deported!"

"You'll have a chance to question the witness when I'm finished," Stanley admonished. He turned to Ashley and asked her to state her full name—Anna Alevtina Sokolov. Such a lengthy freight train of Slavic syllables. No wonder she'd changed it, Kat thought.

"How do you know Ms. Cebu?"

"House sitter."

"Illegal squatter," stage-whispered Vida.

"On August eleventh of last summer, did you reside at Sixty-Six Berry Street?"

"In crummy guest room."

"On more than one occasion, did you witness Ms. Cebu listen to her phone messages?"

"You joke? She check phone machine like fat man check refrigerator."

"And what did these phone messages say?"

"Something smell funny in basement. Help."

Vida looked directly into Kat's eyes, as if she were trying to exercise some kind of hypnotic power over her. "Katherine, please believe me. I never had a chance to hear Edith's messages. I had just gotten back from a trip and found *her* in the closet. I only learned about the mushrooms when the police finally dragged *her* out."

"I don't believe you."

"You believe *her*?"

Stanley intervened to ask Vida's counsel if she had any questions for the witness.

"You bet I do. What did you do to my son? He's now scared of the dark, scared of strangers, scared of loud noises."

"She's not on trial," Stanley said.

"She should be."

Vida rose from her chair and set her hands flat on the table, whether for support or for emphasis Kat wasn't sure.

"Katherine, I'm sorry for your loss. I don't know what else I can say but I'm sorry, so sorry that Edith died. If you want to sue me, so be it. I have nothing left. I lost everything too. Edith's gone. I can't go back in time and change that. You can't blame me for an act of God. I hope you find it in your heart to forgive me. I hope you find some peace."

After Vida and her counsel left, Kat asked everyone if she could have a few minutes alone in the library. She was hoping Edith's spirit would visit. What a quiet room to have spent forty years in. Maybe the quiet was Edith's spirit. Are you here? Is the silence your answer?

Should I forgive her, Edie?

Ashley had almost fled the library when Virginia threatened to have her deported, but she stuck to her story and stayed loyal to Kat. Now she feared she was going to be shipped back to Omsk.

She sat beside Kat and Frank in a Brooklyn-bound taxi. When they stopped for a red light, she considered opening the passenger door and vanishing, but she couldn't stand to be invisible ever again. She liked that Kat refused to believe she was fated for a crummy life making babies. She liked having a Polish cook and a cat. She loved her room; she'd never had one before.

The Syzmanskis and Gladys were waiting for them when Kat unlocked the front door.

"Did she apologize?"

"Did she confess?"

"Did you forgive her?"

Ashley went straight to her room, but when she shut the cat out, she heard its claws relentlessly scraping at the door, *she should be deported, deported, deported.* She must leave immediately, but instead she lay down on her bed in her new dress and pulled up the covers.

It wasn't yet dark. The weak light stranded her few possessions in obscurity—the plastic laptop on the bureau, the penthouse's napkin used as a doily. Through the house's thin walls, she heard the din of camaraderie coming from the living room as everyone made a fuss over Kat and forgot about Ashley.

She didn't want to become Anushka again. How could her eighteen-year-old life already be over?

Hurling off the covers, she rose, smoothed the wrinkles from her satin dress, mounted her platform heels, and clacked into the living room. "I be deported because I help you," she told Kat.

"I won't let that happen."

"Impossible help me."

"She's right," said Mr. Syzmanski. "I had a cousin who had lived in Jersey for forty years when he got deported. He had an American wife and kids, but they never officially got married because he also had a wife and kids back in Poland."

"What does this have to do with Ashley?" asked his wife.

"They weren't a legal family. You have to have a relative who's a U.S. citizen."

"I alone," said Ashley, hunching on the sofa beside Kat.

"You're not alone."

She felt a gentle touch lift her chin until she was looking into Kat's smiling face. Kat's two front teeth were bigger and brighter than anything else Ashley had to guide her.

"You *do* have a family in this country. I'll adopt you," said Kat.

Clearing the dinner dishes, Ashley accidentally dropped a greasy spoon on her lap. She went straight to her room, peeled off her dress, inside out, like a latex glove, and then rushed to the bathroom to submerge it in soapy hot water. She held the stain under the steaming faucet even when her fingertips burned. Could Kat really adopt her?

After hanging the dress over the tub to dry, she returned to her room, leaving the door ajar for the cat, but when she woke just before dawn, the cat wasn't there. Gyrating blue beams danced around her dark room. Naked, she rose from the warm covers and peered out the window. A squad car and a windowless van were parked not twenty feet away. Even before the loud knocking rattled the front door, she dropped to her knees and crawled to the bathroom on the house's far side. Slipping on her still-damp dress, she was about to steal out the window when she heard Kat shout, "Who are you looking for?"

"This is not your business, ma'am, please step away from the door."

"The door you're pounding on is mine, so it is my business."

"We are looking for Anna Alevtina Sokolov."

"I want to see a warrant."

Silence prevailed while Kat read the warrant.

"There is no one by that name living here."

Ashley was halfway out the window when she spotted a bearish man wearing a vest that said ICE POLICE. His flashlight beam caught her just as she leapt.

"Immigration and Customs Enforcement. Stop!"

She started to run in her bare feet, but the ground was mined with broken glass. Her right heel got punctured. The policeman caught her. Not only did he handcuff her, he shackled a chain around her waist.

"Are the *chains* really necessary?" asked Kat.

"Until she's cleared by Homeland Security, yes," said the officer.

"You think she's hiding explosives under that dress?" asked Frank. He, Gladys, the Syzmanskis, and the cat now crowded the stoop.

"She's shivering, for pity's sake," said Kat. "Frank, go get her coat and boots."

Just before Ashley was shoved through the van doors, Frank ran over with her coat and boots. While he helped her into her boots, Kat draped the coat over her shivering shoulders.

"Where are you taking her?"

"What is your relationship to this girl?"

"I'm in the process of adopting her."

"The Elizabeth Detention Center."

"We'll get you out, Ashley, don't worry," promised Kat as the van's rear door shut. There were no windows. The darkness was absolute. The crypt began rolling. About fifteen minutes later, it stopped and the engine was cut. She heard shouting. Someone or something was thrown against the van's side. A police siren wailed. When the rear door finally opened, six Mexicans were pushed inside.

In the dark, Ashley listened for clues as to where she was going—a bridge's clang and clank, bullying horns, a swishing echo, an eardrum pop, a distant jet. About an hour later, the van stopped again, and the doors opened to reveal a brightly lit, windowless, three-square-block, one-story brick warehouse, bigger than any gulag she'd ever seen. The humped roof was crowned with razor wire.

Inside looked like a dog pound—cement floor, rows of wire cages. A female ICE officer led Ashley to a crowded cell in the women's section.

There was nowhere to sit down. She lost track of time. The fluorescents hissed and sparked. Her freed wrists still chafed from the cuffs. She hitched up her red dress and peed in a drain, then sat on the cold floor and employed her bitten fingernails to excise the glass shard from her throbbing right heel.

She was fingerprinted, photographed, showered, de-loused, issued an orange jumpsuit, and then led into a dark dormitory stacked with sleeping, moaning, crying, praying women.

She found an empty cot, the bottom in a stack of three. The mattress gave like a hammock. The pillow's batting smelled of foreign breath. The blanket was thinner than her old beach towel.

A voice whispered to her in Spanish.

"Russian," Ashley said.

"Where are you from?" someone called to her in a Siberian accent.

"Omsk."

"No, I mean which detention center are you from? My sister was supposed to be transferred here from LaSalle. We got separated but we're supposed to be deported together. ICE has to find three hundred and fifty Russians before the plane can leave."

"How long have you been waiting?"

"Six months."

Wearing only a thin robe and slush-sodden slippers, Kat stood on the curb shouting at the receding van, "I'll get you out, Ashley! Hang in there!"

"She can't hear you," said Frank. "Come inside, Kat, you'll catch pneumonia." She allowed herself to be led back into the warm house.

"Blackie and I will pray for her," said Gladys, picking up the cat.

"The kid must be so scared," said Mrs. Syzmanski.

"I should have listened to her. I knew I should have moved her to a hotel last night," said Kat.

It wasn't yet dawn. Everyone went back to their room. Kat left an urgent message on Stanley's office voicemail to call her back no matter the hour. "Should I try his house?" she asked Frank.

"Let the guy sleep. There's nothing anyone can do until morning."

She joined him under the covers and nestled against his warmth, but she spared him her cold feet.

"She didn't have to help me this afternoon, Frank. She could have refused to testify after Vida's lawyer threatened her with deportation, but she bravely told the truth. She knew what that woman was capable of. She'd already thrown

Ashley out on the streets once before. She's eighteen years old, for god's sake. What kind of human being is so vengeful that she would have a teenager arrested in the middle of the night and deported?"

Frank had fallen asleep, his arm heavy on her shoulder. She tried to lull herself to sleep too, but her thoughts wandered back to the quiet library after everyone had left this afternoon. While she had been struggling with mercy and forgiveness, Vida's lawyer had already called immigration. How else could they have gotten here so fast? Vida must have known. Maybe it was Vida who called? How could she have asked to be forgiven and then gone ahead and done this?

Kat had so many questions. She reached for her new smartphone on the nightstand. It was hardly the wise advice giver of yesteryear, but it was all she had.

"What can I help you with?" asked the phone.

"How do I adopt a foreign national?" she whispered into the tiny microphone so as not to wake Frank.

"Let me check that," said the phone. "Would you like me to search the web for 'How do I adopt a foreign national'?"

"Yes."

Every link showed a young couple embracing an infant.

"How old is too old to adopt?"

"The cutoff age is fifty," answered the phone.

"Look up images for the Elizabeth Detention Center."

A windowless warehouse festooned with razor wire filled the screen.

"How do I sponsor a foreign national already in custody?"

"I don't know what you mean. Why do you want to sponsor a foreign national already in custody?" asked the phone. "Would you like me to search the web for 'How do I sponsor a foreign national already in custody'?"

"Yes."

Every link led to another link.

"Who qualifies for amnesty?"

Who qualifies to be forgiven?

At nine sharp the next morning, without having gotten a wink of sleep, she called Stanley's office, but Janice told her that he was in court all day. "How are you holding up after yesterday, Kat?"

"I'm fine, I'm calling about Ashley." She told Janice what had happened. "I've been doing research all night. If she stands a chance of being released, Stanley needs to file Form I-864 and draft an Affidavit of Support granting me the right to sponsor her. I'll also need an affidavit from the trust proving I have the financial means. We have to hurry. She can be deported at any time."

"You sound just like your sister. Edith was always telling Stanley what to do."

At noon, Kat went to bed with a splitting headache and a chill. Frank closed the blinds, but she still couldn't sleep, though she lost track of time. When she next checked the alarm clock, the hands read four, though a.m. or p.m. she wasn't sure. Frank was napping beside her, or maybe he'd been sleeping there all night. Had Stanley left a voicemail? Had Ashley been given her one phone call and Kat had missed it?

No one had called.

The next time she opened her eyes, her lashes produced a swish like high grass blowing in a gale. Lightning branched whether or not her eyes were open or closed, a cyclone of brilliance. She could see the shimmering tornado simulta-neously from all sides, as if a storm posed before a three-way mirror. Was she having a migraine? Edith had suffered them, though until now, she'd been spared.

Just as abruptly as the headache began, the pounding quit. She could hear herself think again. But no thoughts came. She listened for her internal voice but the silence was absolute. All she heard were the inhalations and exhalations her throat made with each involuntary breath. She had never been so alone with herself before.

Frank was less than six inches away, but when she tried to call his name, her tongue slapped against her teeth. She tried to shake him awake, but her arm was gone. If she hadn't been able to see the flaccid limb beside her, she'd have thought her whole arm was only a memory.

Summoning the last of her strength, she managed to swing her torso until her dead arm lassoed against his chest.

Only when she saw his frightened, confused expression did she panic, if one could be said to panic in utter stasis.

"Kat, what's wrong? Say something, you're scaring me."

A bubble rose from her open lips as she struggled to construct a word. A speech balloon?

He leaned closer, his ear to her mouth.

She'd forgotten how to speak.

"Don't leave me, Kat. Stay with me, please. I can't be alone."

He phoned for help, then returned to bed and stretched out against her. He wrapped his arms under and over her useless body and held her as tightly and securely as he could, so her soul couldn't escape.

She recognized the paramedics, the same two seasoned men who had come for Edith, though they didn't appear to remember her. The skinnier of the two aimed a penlight into her pupil. The brilliance was so excruciating, the beam might as well have been a knitting needle. The next thing she remembered was being hoisted onto a gurney and strapped down, like a log on a flatbed truck. Frank wasn't allowed to ride in the ambulance with her. They weren't related. He took her hand and squeezed. She felt nothing.

Maybe she was dead? But if she was dead, wouldn't Edith come find her?

Anushka's arrest met the quota of Russian deportees needed to fill a chartered plane bound for Volgograd. She was handed back her new dress, winter coat, and boots, and put on a plane in the dead of night. At least she had the window seat. She'd only flown once before, nine months ago when she and her red suitcase had traveled to America. Unlike the first flight, this one didn't have any stewardesses to demonstrate how to fasten a seat belt. Two armed guards were posted at either end of the cabin and no one trundled colas and peanuts and pretzels down the aisle.

Until the plane door closed, her fisted heart clung to the shredding hope that Kat could still save her. After the plane took off, she started to despair. The lights of New York City were now passing below her, as if millions and millions of stars had fallen out of the night heavens. Would she ever come back? What if she never did? She could feel her pan-icked heart trying to punch free of her tight dress.

Then the curvature of the earth grew saturated with red, as if a knife had sliced the night in two. Dawn bloomed over the eastern horizon. Her mood began to lift with the young sun. Just because she was being sent back to Russia didn't mean that Kat couldn't adopt her. Look at all those Chinese babies with American mothers. Kat wouldn't let her down. She hadn't let Kat down. Kat probably had no idea where she was. No one let her make a phone call before she was marched onto the plane. She'd call Kat as soon as she landed.

The plane was flying straight into a new day. The sun broke through the sea's surface and rose faster than a bubble in water. The red quickly diluted into pink, and then orange, yellow, flax, straw, and soon it was colorless. Dawn's promise was over before it started. At this speed, she would be back in Russia in no time. She felt despondent again. Who would be waiting for her when she landed? No one.

The plane had been flying only three, four hours when the sun began its descent behind her. How could the day already be over? Clouds cluttered the western horizon, their tips flaming. Mauve and pink vapors crisscrossed the sky. Where the sky and the sea kissed looked tooled in gold and silver. Then, just as fast as a coin drops into a wishing well, the sun fell into the sea and the world lost all color.

The absolute darkness that followed made daylight seem a feeble child's fantasy. She tried to sleep. The plane bounced and trembled, as if it had run over a body.

What time was it? What if the adoption took years?

She was hyperventilating in her tight dress. To catch her breath, she loosened her seat belt and looked out the window. And there it was, another dawn, with all its expectant hope.

The plane landed in Volgograd. Anushka was given a train ticket to the city of her birth, Omsk, courtesy of the U.S. government.

She hadn't eaten in two days when she pounded on her parents' door.

"Anushka?" stammered her father, hugging and kissing

his eldest daughter. Her siblings swarmed behind him, gawking at their big sister in her expensive American winter coat and boots.

"Did you bring us any presents?" they begged.

"Wasn't your contract for a year?" her mother asked.

When she took off her coat, everyone gaped at her red satin dress, everyone except her mother.

"Where is the suitcase we bought you?"

Her father went to buy Anushka's favorite food, smoked sausages. Her mother served them with stewed cabbage in a big communal bowl. The family crowded around the kitchen table. In honor of her return, the ancient tablecloth had been laid out, with its family history of stains. Her siblings didn't wait for the guest of honor. Even before her parents finished their prayers of thanks for her safe return, her brothers' forks were aimed and ready.

"Did you meet anyone famous?" her sisters wanted to know. "Can we try on your red dress?"

"You look so American," her father marveled.

"Did you save any money? Are you planning on getting a job? Do you want me to talk to someone at the factory?" asked her mother.

She could feel her shoulders slowly hunching, her spine already starting to slouch.

"If you're not going to eat that sausage . . . ," said her elder brother.

By the time dinner was over, her novelty had worn off and the family watched TV. She waited for her parents to go to bed, and then slipped into the kitchen to use the ancient dial phone. The room's smell, at once so familiar and suffocating, almost made her cry. The neighbors' living room window looked directly into their kitchen. A girl she remembered from high school stood rocking a screaming baby. She dialed zero, dragging the rotary dial all the way around. She'd forgotten how heavy it was.

"I want to make a collect call," she whispered to the operator so as not to wake her parents in the next room.

Oh, please, Kat, answer. She heard Kat's voice. "It me," she whispered before she realized she'd only reached voice-mail.

"There's no one home to accept the charges," confirmed the operator.

"I'll pay for the call."

"Kat, I in Omsk," she told the voicemail. "Call back. Please." She changed her mind. The ring would only wake her parents, who might not approve of someone else adopting her. "Don't call. I email you."

She took money from her mother's purse and walked to the internet café where her old gang used to hang out, an ex-nightclub with smoky blue lights. She used to think it was so sophisticated. It now looked gaudy and shabby at the same time. She was thankful she recognized no one. She'd told her old gang she was never coming back.

i in omsk help me i nead tiket four jet to ny i wate ear frum u, she typed on the relic of a computer.

She couldn't wait too long for a reply at ten rubles a minute. What time was it in New York?

where r u, she typed.

Maybe she had the wrong email address? But she knew her own street address. The next morning, she asked her mother for a pen and paper.

"Who you writing to in America?" her mother wanted to know.

"Mama, I'm going back. Another family wants me."

Never let this happen to me was all Vida could think when she saw Kat now shrunk to half size in less than a month. A pillow had been fluffed and positioned so that Kat could see out without having to support her head, if that cloudy blue eye, opaque as an opalescent marble, could still see. The other eyelid was taped shut. Monitors, pumps, tubes, and lines were plugged into both the wall sockets and her veins. A hooked bag of fluid swelled beneath her bed, as if the tiny immobile mass under the snowy white hospital sheet were melting.

Bright, festive floral displays filled every available surface in the tiny room. The half-dozen daisies Vida had quickly chosen from the hospital gift shop looked meager by comparison.

Frank occupied the room's only chair.

"How is she doing?" Vida asked.

"How does it look like she's doing? She had a stroke. She had the same fungal pneumonia that Edith did, but the doctor said we got her here in time. He said she probably had the spores in her lungs all along, but her immune system kept them in check until now. Don't say anything to upset her," Frank warned. "She's been through enough already." He vacated his chair, but he stood just outside the door, leaving Vida alone with Kat.

The cloudy blue eye swiveled in Vida's direction as she stepped closer to the bed. Was there a consciousness in there, or was the pupil involuntarily tracking her motions? Kat's shrunken countenance gave nothing away. The two halves of her face told two entirely different stories—the left side spoke of strain and bafflement, the right, with its taped eyelid, of lethargy and slack. Suddenly, the taped eye began struggling against its bondage while the free eye sharpened, as if someone had polished it. Vida didn't need to wonder any longer. There was a fully conscious human being on the other side of the glass.

"Kat, is there anything I can get you? Would you like some water?" She glanced out the window. "Spring is almost here. I just stopped by to bring you these daisies and see how you're doing. I'll let you get some rest now."

In all her years of acting, she had never been watched with such steadfast concentration. Milky liquid began slowly leaking from the resolute, fixated blue stare.

Vida wasn't sure if she should leave to let the poor creature collect herself, or if she should reach for a tissue to blot away the overflow of emotions. The eye valiantly blinked away its own tears and then concentrated on Vida again. The canny intelligence inside appeared to grow brighter, as if the theater's lights had come on and Vida could see her audience.

She forgot her lines.

She forgot her lies.

All she had left was the truth.

"Oh, Kat, I'm sorry, so sorry if anything I did caused your suffering." Her tears were scalding and uncontrollable, and came from an entirely different place than the tears she shed onstage. She leaned closer so that her lips were next to Kat's good ear. Though her heart was sprinting, she spoke slowly so that Kat understood every word. "You were right. I wasn't telling the whole truth. I *did* hear Edith's first message. I *should* have called her back. I have no excuse. No words can express how sorry I am. Please find it in your heart to forgive me."

Kat began thrashing under the covers, as if Vida's confession had gravely agitated her, but once she freed her good hand from the tangled sheet, she became calm again, almost serene. It took an excruciatingly long time, but she managed to raise her hand and rest it on Vida's bowed head. The hand was astonishingly gentle. Vida waited for a sign of absolution, but Kat appeared to have expended all her energy just reaching this high.

When Vida's mother heard that her famous actress daughter hadn't worked in months, except as a towel girl, she sent Vida an airplane ticket home, to Cebu. Her mother's family had a modest ancestral home in Lapu-Lapu City. The last time Vida had visited was during a quick stopover on her way to a Singaporean production of *Cymbeline*. She hadn't seen her mother in almost five years.

The flight lasted eighteen hours by clock, a day and a half by calendar. At least she had the window seat. The plane took off straight into a glorious spring sunset, but two hours later, the sun still waffled on the western horizon. An ever-changing cloud extravaganza put on one performance after another, as if auditioning for the sun's final act. After three hours of the unrelenting spectacle, she shut her window and tried to catch some sleep, but her thoughts restlessly returned to the hospital visit yesterday. Why had Kat forgiven her? That gesture of absolution, if that's what it was, had given Vida no solace. She wished that Kat had slapped her instead. Maybe then she'd be able to sleep.

A tiny Filipina with iron-gray kiss-curls and out-of-date coaster-sized sunglasses approached Vida in the baggage claim area. Only after a jarring second did Vida recognize her mother.

They embraced, her mother fiercely, Vida with tender

caution. She noted her mother's shrinkage, smelled her coconut oil shampoo. Her mother's gray hair had thinned to the point where Vida could see the fragile globe underneath.

"Only one suitcase?" asked her mother after Vida retrieved her frayed, taped, bruised, overnight bag from the conveyor belt, the one she'd been wheeling behind her for the past ten months.

In the sweltering parking lot, a new white Jeep beeped and flashed when her mother clicked the car keys. "Your father's Social Security wouldn't buy me cat food in New York, but here it buys me steak, and an SUV."

Lapu-Lapu, an old fishing village across the causeway from Cebu City, was unrecognizable. Cement resorts had risen like termite mounds along the shoreline. The family's coral-brick one-story home now stood outside the Imperial Palace Waterpark Resort's cyclone fence, barring passage to the beach. But her pragmatic mother found the upside. "God showed me where there was a hole in the fence. I now have a free pool and a hot tub."

As soon as her mother unlocked the Chinese-red door, before she had a chance to show off the new fridge and flat-screen TV to her daughter, Vida begged exhaustion after the long flight and asked to lie down, but as soon as she closed her eyes, she was back at the hospital.

Was she forgiven?

That evening after dinner, while she and her mother sat outside under a crackling blue bug lamp, Vida said, "Something awful happened back in New York, Nanay."

Her mother allowed herself only one cigarette a day, and she lit it now.

"Remember my tenants, the identical twin sisters I told you about?"

"One blond and the other gray."

"Yes. They both got very sick from a mold infestation in my basement. One died."

"You should come to Mass with me tomorrow and beg God's forgiveness."

"I didn't know how toxic the mold was, no one did. It wasn't a normal mold. It was a supermold. According to my insurance company, the infestation was an act of God."

"He's responsible for every living thing, but it doesn't mean you shouldn't beg His forgiveness."

To her mother's dismay at church the next morning, Vida refused to kneel before the priest and accept the sacramental wafer.

"Nanay, I'm happy to come and sit with you in church, but you know I don't believe."

"Even your insurance company believes."

She hadn't told anyone, except Virginia, that she was leaving New York. Was she leaving New York? A fresh start? It was oddly appealing.

Vida's second cousin, who seemed to make a living solely by introducing people, arranged an audition, a guest appearance on a local telenovela, *Angel, Angel.* The part called for a Eurasian to play the star's visiting aunt from America. The cousin told Vida the job was hers as soon as the producer saw the footage.

"What footage? Where did you get a clip of my work?"

"The Ziberax ad."

The audition was a formality. The producer, a blond Filipina a few years older than Vida, only wanted to know if Ziberax worked.

To her surprise, Vida found soap acting's stylized histrionics and ensemble atmosphere not so different from a

Shakespeare company. By the end of the first month, her character, Maria—an extortionist who knows the beauty queen Angel, Angel's secret, that she was switched at birth—had become wildly popular. The producer, now a friend, pleaded with Vida to stay on and promised a fat weekly check. During the next twenty-five episodes, the writers had Maria plot as many murders as Lady Macbeth. The first season was about to end with her poisoning Angel, Angel. Then, out of the blue, Virginia called with a part—two parts, actually, Queen Gertrude and Hermione. The director, Vida's old lover, was reassembling the ensemble for another season in Central Park. The Delacorte Theater had finally been rebuilt.

She told her Filipina producer to have the writers kill off Maria, she wasn't going to do another season.

In the six remaining episodes, a plot twist had Maria drink her own poison and suffer a stroke. The last three shows took place in a hospital room, where Maria lingered long enough to end the season with a teaser. In the last shot on the last day, Vida asked to end her performance with an extreme close-up. She didn't want any help from the makeup department to achieve the droop of paralysis. All she wanted was her right eye taped shut. As the camera moved in for the final shot, Vida opened her good eye. The left half of her face remained unchanged, but the right half drooped as if the musculature underneath had turned to jelly. The taped lid began struggling against its bondage. The good eye stared unblinking into the widening lens, lest the audience forget that a human being was looking back at them from the far side of the glass.

A NOTE ON THE TYPE

This book was set in Adobe Garamond. Designed for the Adobe Corporation by Robert Slimbach, the fonts are based on types first cut by Claude Garamond (ca. 1480–1561). Garamond was a pupil of Geoffroy Tory and is believed to have followed the Venetian models, although he introduced a number of important differences, and it is to him that we owe the letter we now know as "old style." He gave to his letters a certain elegance and feeling of movement that won their creator an immediate reputation and the patronage of Francis I of France.

Typeset by Scribe, Philadelphia, Pennsylvania

Printed and bound by Berryville Graphics,
Berryville, Virginia

Designed by Betty Lew